Her body went to his

A raw sound growled up from the throat as Hannah found his lips and kissed him. His hands wrapped around her, this time with more intent and purpose. She could feel the difference in how he flexed his fingers against her, the added pressure tantalizing her all the more.

"Hannah." He breathed her name against her mouth. "Are you sure?"

"Positive." She gripped his biceps, wanting him inside where she could take his clothes off.

Straightening, she withdrew the key card for the door from the small hip pocket sewn into her leggings. Her fingers were unsteady as she slid it through the reader.

"I don't have protection with me, but my house is just through the woods."

"I have something." A good thing, because she wasn't willing to wait for him to make a trip to his place.

Pushing open the door, she knew stepping over the threshold was a point of no return. But she had no reservations about this, a moment of pleasure in a year of hell. The only things she felt right now were hunger and need...the desire for him so stark she couldn't begin to account for it.

* * *

One Night Scandal is part of the McNeill Magnates series from Joanne Rock!

Dear Reader,

A Hollywood movie is filming on the Creek Spill Ranch, and the Wyoming McNeills are struggling to conduct business as usual with all the extra activity and media attention. And now there's a blackmailer on the loose, determined to reveal the family secrets! Welcome to the last installment of the McNeill Magnates, where we find out the truth of Paige's hidden identity and solve the puzzle of who has been tormenting the McNeills.

But first, there's romance! Because the heat between Brock McNeill and sultry actress Hannah Ryder won't be denied, even though Hannah is keeping secrets of her own. Will Brock see through her? Or will the rugged rancher understand that she's protecting someone close to her?

It's a nonstop ride full of sizzle, and I hope you enjoy every moment of it. Thank you, my friends, for reading the saga of the McNeills, and I hope you'll join me online for giveaways, sneak peeks at future books and more at joannerock.com.

Happy reading,

Joanne Rock

JOANNE ROCK

—

ONE NIGHT SCANDAL

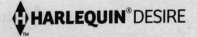

Recycling programs
for this product may
not exist in your area.

ISBN-13: 978-1-335-97174-6

One Night Scandal

Copyright © 2018 by Joanne Rock

Printed in U.S.A.

HARLEQUIN®
www.Harlequin.com

Four-time RITA® Award nominee **Joanne Rock** has penned over seventy stories for Harlequin. An optimist by nature and a perpetual seeker of silver linings, Joanne finds romance fits her life outlook perfectly—love is worth fighting for. A Golden Heart® Award recipient, she has won numerous awards for her stories. Learn more about Joanne's imaginative muse by visiting her website, joannerock.com, or following @joannerock6 on Twitter.

Books by Joanne Rock

Harlequin Desire

The McNeill Magnates

The Magnate's Mail-Order Bride
The Magnate's Marriage Merger
His Accidental Heir
Little Secrets: His Pregnant Secretary
Claiming His Secret Heir
For the Sake of His Heir
The Forbidden Brother
Wild Wyoming Nights
One Night Scandal

Visit her Author Profile page at Harlequin.com, or joannerock.com, for more titles.

To Mandy Lawler for all of your
help and guidance.
Thank you!

One

Hannah Ryder scavenged her last scrap of patience as the film director she despised zoomed in on her for a close-up shot. The bright lights were making her sweat right through the thick layers of makeup. Itchy, dry hay poked her bare skin. She lay smothered in the stuff on the floor of an old barn temporarily transformed into a movie set. The scene called for her character to fall through the loft in the middle of hooking up with a cowboy; thankfully, the stunt had been pulled off by someone else paid to do that sort of thing.

Now, Hannah had to perform the sequence following the fall after her cowboy lover had abandoned her. Her face was covered in cosmetics to look like blood and bruises. All of which was fine, if she hadn't been in her third hour of shooting reaction shots while drowning in hay that made her eyes water and her skin burn. Her makeup had to be retouched every twenty minutes to keep it from sliding off, and the flesh-toned bodysuit she wore under the hay didn't protect her in the least. Horses flanked her on either side, their impatient hooves providing a frame for the scene, according to the sadist in charge. What if one of the animals decided he was tired of a sneezing woman writhing on the floor of his barn?

Twice she was sure a spider or some other creepy-crawly had skittered up her bare leg, and a cramp knotted her calf.

She would have walked off the production days ago if she hadn't wrangled a part in this film for a very specific reason. She needed evidence of the director's sexual harassment of women on the set to help avenge what he'd done to Hannah's younger sister a year ago.

The incident had transformed nineteen-year-old Hope from a bright-eyed aspiring writer, with a coveted job as script reader and assistant to director Antonio Ventura, into a quiet shell of her former self. Hope now worked in retail, content to unlock dressing rooms for customers since it was a job that surrounded her with women. Hope didn't write anymore, and she showed no desire to leave the house for any reason but work. She startled at noises and cried when she thought Hannah couldn't hear.

The change broke Hannah's heart, and months of therapy hadn't seemed to help her sister. Hope refused to file charges, insisting she'd destroyed evidence after the fact because of conflicted feelings, and she didn't want to bring a case she couldn't prove. When months of gentle encouragement and outright coercing had proven ineffective, Hannah had taken a new approach. She'd spend time on one of the bastard's sets to see for herself if he was victimizing other females.

So far all she'd learned was that every single person who worked on his film *Winning the West* thought he was a tyrant and a megalomaniac. But she had no evidence that he was locking vulnerable women in closets to forcibly grope them the way he'd done to Hope.

Just the thought of it steeled Hannah to withstand the cramp throbbing in her calf for another minute while the camera closed in on her tears. She'd been Hope's guardian ever since her sister had moved to Los Angeles to be with Hannah. Their parents had never been much help since their high-powered attorney father had walked out on their mother long ago—taking his family fortune with him. As for their mom, she'd done her best to raise Hope and Hannah, but she'd made no secret of the fact that she was "done" once Hope had turned eighteen.

Hannah would never be "done." And she would fight for her sister even if Hope refused to fight for herself.

A horse snorted and tossed his head, a hoof momentarily pinning Hannah's hair to the floor before shifting away again. She couldn't smother her gasp, ruining the take.

But before the director could explode in rage, a tall, broad-shouldered cowboy stepped into view, casting a long shadow onto the floor where Hannah lay.

"Ventura, I need to take my horses," the man demanded, his tone uncompromising as he confronted the despot in charge of the shoot. "Now."

A murmur of collective surprise—quickly stifled—stirred the production team ringing the small barn.

Hannah stretched quietly in the sea of hay, wanting a better look at the cowboy whose arrival had diverted the director's ire away from her. The newcomer blocked the lights, providing a welcome moment of coolness for her itchy skin.

She craned her neck to see around a horse's knee.

And got an eyeful of feminine fantasy material in denim and worn boots. The hard-muscled cowboy stood a head taller than the director, his biceps straining the fabric of a gray cotton T-shirt as he reached to stroke a hand over a horse's nose.

The man's features remained in shadow, thanks to the set of his dark Stetson, but the sharp edge of his jaw and the hint of dark hair curling along the collar of his shirt were enough to make any woman long to see more. For now, Hannah settled on taking in the rest of him, from where his shirt tapered along his back, from his formidable shoulders down to his lean hips.

"You are ruining my shot," Antonio Ventura snapped at the cowboy, his dark eyes narrowing. "Now, thanks to you, I'll need the animals even longer."

The fury brewing under the quiet words made the sweat on Hannah's back turn cold and clammy, worry chilling her.

"Whether you need them or not isn't my concern." The cowboy took the reins of the one closest to him. "They're not professional actors, and they're done for today."

Hannah would have admired anyone unafraid to stand up to a bully like Ventura. But she took a special brand of pleasure in seeing this big, strong guy put the smarmy brute in his place.

"As you can see—" Ventura enunciated each word as if the cowboy was a simpleton "—they are hardly being asked to act. They're standing in the middle of a barn, just the same as they will be when you take them with you. I suggest you consult your boss before you make a choice that will cost you your job."

The dirtbag. How unfair to threaten the man's livelihood. Hannah was already mentally composing a letter to the ranch owner in the cowboy's defense.

"My choice is made." The sexy stranger gathered the other horse's reins in the opposite hand. "And since we're making suggestions, I'm going to advise you to take better care of your actors." The man's gaze fell to where Hannah sprawled in the hay. "Do you need a hand, miss?"

His eyes were blue. Clear sky blue.

Wide-open spaces, Wyoming blue.

Hannah wanted to fall right into them.

Except, she realized, she couldn't afford to thumb her nose at Antonio Ventura before she'd gathered evidence of his criminal behavior. With more than a little regret, she shook her head, a stray piece of hay poking the back of her neck as she moved.

"No. Thank you." She risked a small smile at the horseman, hoping the director was too busy seething to notice.

When she gave her boss a quick glance, he seemed to be pounding out digits on his cell phone as he paced away from the camera equipment.

"You're going to regret this show of stupidity," Ventura threatened between clenched teeth.

Around him, the production team buzzed with new life, sensing they were done shooting for the day as the cowboy guided the animals out of the wide barn door. The night air rushed in.

Hannah watched his retreat, her breath stuck in her chest as she followed his long-legged stride, an easy swagger that made her wish she would have accepted his hand when he'd offered it. What might it have been like to touch him? To keep that blue gaze trained on her a little longer?

Behind her, the wardrobe stylist cleared her throat. "Um… Hannah?"

Swiveling away from the enticing view, Hannah glanced up to find the young woman holding a robe in her hands.

"Sorry. I must have gotten distracted." She grinned conspiratorially as a production assistant shut off the hottest of the set lights nearby. Hannah didn't want anyone to see how stressed this shoot was making her. Her muscles were cramped from the strain and tension of working with her sister's molester as much as from holding the twisted pose for hours.

"Didn't we all?" the stylist, Callie, agreed. Her high, dark ponytail swung in front of her narrow shoulders as she leaned down to wrap the cover-up around Hannah, shielding her in the flesh-tone bodysuit. "I think I forgot to breathe just now."

The woman's vanilla fragrance settled around Hannah as surely as the silk dressing robe. Hannah's itchiness eased immediately from the fresh air, the cooler temperature without the set lights and being free of the hay.

She was stepping into the leather slides that Callie had brought out for her when, from the other side of a rolling cart stuffed full of electronics, a series of shouted curse words blistered her ears. Callie flinched and Hannah's eye started to twitch while they listened to the director yell at whoever was on the other end of the call.

Hannah needed to get away from here. Three hours of dealing with that man was more than she could take. She had a private cabin on-site at the Creek Spill Ranch, close to where filming took place each day. No need to stay here and listen to Ventura's tirade when her accommodations were within walking distance.

"Callie, I think I'm going to call it a night and head back to my room," she said softly, tying the belt on her robe. It was blousy and pretty enough to pass for a caftan. "I can take off my own makeup."

"I don't blame you," the stylist muttered under her breath, her gaze moving furtively toward their boss. He looked ready to pop the vein in his temple, his face contorting as he shouted about ineptitude in his staff and incompetence in the production company. "Take some makeup wipes," Callie said, passing a small plastic packet before gesturing to Hannah's face. "You don't want anyone to think you've just been in a horrible accident."

Hannah was already peeling out a damp cloth from the pack. "You're a lifesaver." Retrieving her purse from behind one of the barn columns, she headed for the door, leather shoes slapping the bottoms of her sockless feet. "Thanks, Callie. I'll see you in the morning."

Part of her wondered if she should stick around a little longer while Ventura was all worked up and angry in case the bad mood brought his criminal tendencies out. But she was physically exhausted, her spirit weary after the trying day. She needed to de-stress tonight. Conserve some energy for tomorrow.

She'd take a soak in the tub. Maybe try some yoga. The porch of her tiny, secluded cabin had a beautiful view during the day. And at night, she could see stars for miles. But as she hurried across the ranch to indulge herself in some much needed downtime, an image of her sister's tearful face returned to chastise her.

Back home, Hope wouldn't be de-stressing tonight. And she sure as hell wasn't taking any feminine joy from admiring the way a brash cowboy looked in jeans.

Priorities quickly realigning, Hannah double-timed her steps toward the cabin. She'd shower, change and sneak back over to the barn to see what else Antonio the Ass got up to tonight. Because nothing would give her more pleasure than putting him behind bars.

Not even a diversion with the sexy horseman who'd rescued her from the shoot today.

Brock McNeill couldn't get the actress out of his mind.

Two hours after he'd removed his quarter horses from the set of the idiot director who was making life at the Creek Spill Ranch a living hell, Brock was more than a little preoccupied by thoughts of the curvy blonde covered in hay. There was something about her that appealed to him—something far more intriguing than her looks, although she was easy enough on the eyes even with the heavy blue and purple makeup meant to look like bruising.

Now, riding back through a rocky ravine to his place after a late consultation with the vet, he found his thoughts on the woman instead of on his sick filly. As the head of the quarter horse breeding and development program at the Creek Spill Ranch, Brock realized his focus needed to be on his portion of the family business now more than ever. The film shoot required it. But the timing couldn't be worse.

Because the McNeills were bracing for a scandal. A blackmailer had promised to reveal his stepmother's secrets to the world two days from now. The whole Wyoming branch of the family was on high alert, waiting for the other shoe to drop because they'd decided not to meet the blackmailer's demands.

To make matters worse, Brock's stepmother was still recovering from a suspicious hiking accident that had put her in a coma right around the time the blackmailer had first surfaced. It was a mess.

Brock needed to protect his family. As the youngest of his brothers, born after the twins Carson and Cody, Brock had always been the odd-man out. It had been easy to fly under the radar in a big family, but the time had come to step up and prove himself now that his brothers needed to focus on their own relationships. Plus, his half sisters were particularly vulnerable because the blackmailer was hinting that their mother's marriage to Donovan McNeill was invalid. Brock needed to be there for his father, his stepmother and his half sisters.

So it was flat-out wrong for him to spend his mental energy thinking about the hay-strewn beauty on the floor of his barn. Dating an actress would only draw more attention to his family when they needed to lay low. It was bad enough his sister Scarlett had been in the tabloids recently for dating one of the film's lead actors. Besides, thinking about the woman so much was crazy, considering he'd watched her work for only half an hour or so. He'd shown up at the shoot because the ranch hands tasked with bringing the horses back hadn't returned. Brock didn't appreciate having his generosity with his animals taken advantage of, so he'd gone to set Antonio Ventura straight for himself. And gotten distracted by the woman crying tears that looked all too real.

She'd only been performing, of course. He understood that. But the tears had gone right through him, the pain in her eyes so damn convincing it had been tough to look away. What made a woman choose a job so emotionally demanding? Because—performing or not—tears like that didn't manufacture themselves. They came from somewhere deep. Seeing her like that had felt oddly intimate.

Maybe that's all it was. He'd caught a stranger in a moment that felt intensely private. Except then she'd smiled at him. The smallest twitch of her lips when their eyes met, and there'd been…

Heat.

He would swear from the look in her eyes that he hadn't been the only one feeling a connection.

Brock decided to circle back to the remote barn Ventura had been shooting in earlier, wanting to see for himself that the guy had released the actress from work. Because while Brock had succeeded in freeing his horses from the director's overheated set, he hadn't gotten the satisfaction of witnessing the blonde walk away from the grueling job. He'd rather lift bales of hay all day than spend an hour sitting in the stuff half-naked the way she had. Especially the old, super-dry variety the director had spread all over the floor. Brock guessed a bed of nails would be more comfortable.

Reining in his horse as he reached the old, small barn that had outlived its usefulness on the ranch, Brock could see filming must have stopped since the lights were dim. A damn good thing, since he would be well within his rights as a partial owner of the McNeill lands to shut down filming if the company violated safety protocols, a clause his brother Carson had the sense to put into the contract with the production company. And working in a wood barn with hot lights and overheated straw that could catch fire veered into dangerous terrain.

The doors were open, though, inviting bears and other foragers inside. Someone must have forgotten to close up for the night. Swinging down from the mare, he patted her neck before dropping the reins and stepping through the open wood doors.

A dark shadow emerged from behind a support post.

A curvy shadow.

Brock recognized the shape of her instantly. No mean feat considering she'd been mostly covered in straw the last time he'd seen her. Apparently, his imagination had done a highly accurate job of filling in the blanks where her body was concerned.

She was dressed in dark leggings and a dark T-shirt. Her platinum hair was tucked under a ball cap with the logo of a West Coast football team. With her face scrubbed clean of makeup, he could see her features better now. The long lashes over her eyes. A few freckles on her nose. Then the stubborn tilt to her chin as she spotted him just inside the barn entrance.

"I sure hope you're off the clock at this hour." Brock summoned a smile, not wanting to startle her when she was alone. "I came back to make sure your director knew enough to call it a day."

She shuffled from one tennis shoe to the other. Was she uneasy?

He took a side step to lean against the barn door, giving her plenty of space to walk out if she chose.

She folded her arms across her chest and stood her ground instead.

"So did I," she claimed, although something vaguely defensive about the way she said it made him wonder if that was true. "I walked off the set right after you did, but the director was in such a snit, I returned because I wanted to make sure he wasn't—" She took a deep breath and let it back out as if she was forcing herself to relax. "Taking advantage of people with no seniority."

Her careful phrasing seemed…off. She was hiding something, and it didn't take a genius to see she was uncomfortable. Maybe he'd been mistaken about the attraction before. Maybe it had been all one-sided.

"That would make him even more of an ass than I already took him for," Brock said, preparing to leave, in case he was responsible for her feeling uneasy. Straightening from the doorframe, he was about to wish her a good-night when her laugh caught him off guard.

A genuine laugh. Surprise music to his ears.

Some of his tension eased as hers seemed to.

"He is. Most definitely." She took a step closer to him, a smile lighting up her whole face, transforming her from pretty to breathtaking. "I'm Hannah Ryder, by the way."

She extended her hand. Anticipation flared at the thought of touching her.

"Brock. It's a pleasure to meet you." He closed his fingers around hers and squeezed.

His hand lingered for a moment longer than necessary. Just enough to see her notice. Her pupils widened a fraction. She sucked in a quick breath.

Gratified that he hadn't been wrong about their first meeting—that there was something hot lurking just beneath the surface between them—he released her hand. He hadn't mentioned his last name, preferring to avoid the inevitable interest in his well-known, wealthy family. Brock had been down that road before, not realizing a woman he'd cared about had been after him only for the connections. The McNeill lifestyle. Or, more accurately, other McNeills' lifestyle. Brock preferred hard work to jet-setting, no matter that his hotel magnate grandfather owned five-star resorts all over the world.

Hannah Ryder toyed with the long sleeve of her dark T-shirt, pulling it over one hand, but not before he spotted a silver ring in the shape of an eternity knot. "I didn't get the chance to thank you earlier, but your entrance was very well timed."

There was a slight husky quality to her voice that made the sound as warm and inviting as a whiskey shot. She was about a head shorter than him, maybe a little more. Dressed all in black with her hair tucked under the cap, she looked like she was trying to avoid recognition. Maybe movie people dressed that way all the time when they were off duty. She seemed about as far from his idea of a diva as possible.

"I regret that I didn't intervene sooner, before my horse's hoof landed on your hair." He couldn't act fast enough after that, knowing the animals were too restless to be trusted standing so close to her head. "You barely even winced."

She shrugged, shaking her head. "But it was enough to ruin another shot. Whenever I let my guard down even a little bit, then it's my fault the whole crew gets stuck on the set for an extra hour."

"Is it always like this?" He realized her eyes were gray under the shadow of her cap's brim.

She smelled good, too. Like soap and wildflowers. He caught the hint of fragrance as she played with the shirtsleeve, the fabric rubbing against her skin.

"Not at all. My job is usually pretty fun, but this film is making me see how much the director has to do with setting a production's tone."

Brock wanted to ask her more, but he guessed she must be tired after her long day.

"Well, for what it's worth, I thought you were fantastic today." He wasn't overstating it, or flattering her. She was good. "In fact, it was because I was so caught up in watching your performance that I didn't interrupt filming sooner."

She laughed again, the sound another surprise shot of pure adrenaline.

"So I have no one to blame but myself for my hair getting stepped on? Are you saying that if I'd been a worse actress, you would have come to the rescue sooner?" Her gray eyes twinkled with mischief.

Teasing. Flirtation.

It wasn't a game Brock had played often. Or well. But he damned well recognized it.

He let the new flames crackle through him, stunned that a total stranger could stir that level of heat. What was it about her? Hell, what was it about *him* that he was letting it draw him in?

"I'm saying, Hannah Ryder, that you're not an easy woman to look away from."

He heard the tone of his voice; it was all wrong for the moment. It brought the teasing and flirtation to a halt. The air around them changed. Got warmer.

He saw the confusion in her gaze. The surprise. A whole host of emotions flickered through her expression that he couldn't identify.

But there was one that he knew. Because he felt it, too.

Desire.

It pulsed in the charged air like a heartbeat. For a moment, he thought she might take a step toward him. Until, outside the barn, his horse whinnied softly. Breaking the moment and the connection.

"I'd better go." She tucked her chin into her chest and stalked past him. Out of the barn and into the night.

Brock watched her leave, knowing he shouldn't follow. She'd made her decision. He respected that. He needed to check in with his family anyhow, see if their investigator had any updates on the blackmailer.

Taking a deep, cooling breath to ward off the lingering hunger for Hannah, he took his time stepping outside. Only to glimpse her outline in the moonlight.

With her back to him, he could see clearly the image that she'd pulled up on her phone.

A map of the ranch.

Walking directions back to her cabin.

Brock closed his eyes for a long moment, knowing he couldn't let her make the long trek in the dark by herself. He would give his own sisters a hard time about navigating those woods on foot alone at night, and they'd been raised here, fully aware of what to look out for. How much did a West Coast visitor understand about the potential dangers of the Wyoming land?

Steeling himself against the inevitable draw of the woman, Brock stepped closer to make an offer that was going to be hell on his restraint.

"How about I give you a ride home?"

Two

The cowboy's voice smoked through her, heating her insides and sending a shiver of awareness over Hannah's skin.

Did she want a ride?

Her subconscious was going to have way too much fun tormenting her with that image in her dreams tonight. For now, she needed to stop fantasizing about sexy Brock, the rancher who turned her inside out with just a handful of words and a smoldering gaze.

Her legs were still unsteady after whatever it was that had passed between them inside the barn. She'd had meaningful relationships in her past. Men she'd loved. And yet no one had ever given her the sizzling shock to the system that she felt from being around this stranger. Swallowing hard, she braced herself as she turned around to refuse his offer.

"That's okay. I don't mind walking." Her voice was soft and breathless when she needed it to be firm and sure. "I, um, could use the fresh air."

She could also use a new libido. One that wasn't quite so susceptible to tall, muscular cowboys. It must be because of all the stress she was under with her sister. She'd latched on to a pleasurable distraction and now she couldn't quite let go.

Brock folded his arms across his impressive chest. God, his arms were amazing, too. She wanted to skim her hands up the triceps and over his shoulders. Instead, she jammed her restless fingers in the back pockets of her jeans along with her phone.

"You'd probably be fine," he acknowledged. "You must have walked over here in the dark in the first place, although the moon was higher at that hour, making the path a lot easier to follow than it will be now."

She had been thinking the same thing since she didn't remember exactly where she'd broken through the brush to find the barn. Nightfall in this part of Wyoming was nothing like it was in Southern California. Here, there was no ambient light of any kind. Just deep blackness and stars.

"I've got my phone," she argued, although she was beginning to wonder what else might be out there in the wilderness surrounding the ranch lands. She'd heard wolves—or some kind of wild dogs—baying in the distance on the walk over here. "The cabin I'm staying in is just through there."

She pointed vaguely, trying to see any kind of trail.

"I'm not sure calling someone will do you any good if you meet up with a bear. Or an elk. Or some other wild animal that wasn't expecting company at this hour."

She didn't want to be foolish. So, in spite of the out-of-control attraction, she figured the best thing to do would be to accept the ride and get home as fast as possible.

And put this encounter out of her mind.

"Is your truck nearby?" she asked, peering around the barn. During the shoot, there'd been a couple of golf carts and two trucks parked there.

A smile curved that hard mouth of his. Nodding, he relaxed his arms and walked past her, close enough for her to feel the warmth of his body, close enough for his sleeve to brush hers.

"My horse is right this way."

"Horse?" Her belly flipped.

Not because she minded riding a horse. Only because it implied a proximity that...

A shiver stole over her skin. Her nerve endings danced in anticipation of touching him. Something her brain knew was a very, very bad idea.

"I—" Her voice wasn't even there. She licked her lips. Tried again. "I'm not sure—"

"You'll be fine," he assured her, holding a hand out for her while he stood next to a dark horse with a glossy coat. "I'll help you up." He flipped the ring for her foot so it was easier for her to see. "Step into the stirrup and you'll be home in no time."

Her heart pounded a chaotic, fast beat. But stalling wasn't going to get her home any faster. She understood that much. Willing herself to remain calm, she stabbed the toe of her tennis shoe through the foothold.

Brock's hands were quick and efficient as he boosted her up onto the saddle. He didn't linger. But he might as well have been massaging her naked body for how her skin reacted under her clothes. Her thigh tingled. Her waist...

She wanted his hands there again. Before she could gather herself or prepare for more, Brock swung up onto the animal behind her. His chest was against her back. Her hips tucked into the cradle of his lap, his strong thighs bracketing hers.

There was no space. No distance. And it felt so good she couldn't have spoken if she'd tried. The only thing she didn't like about it was that she shouldn't like it so damn much.

But there was no chance to protest now as his arm curled around her waist, his hand bracing her protectively against him while he nudged the animal into motion. Hannah sucked in a gasp at the feel of their bodies moving together. In sync. Rubbing together.

It was the most erotic experience of her life, and she hardly knew the man. Keenly aware of his body, Hannah closed her eyes to try to shut out the feel of him…everywhere. But even that proved dangerous, as her mind vividly supplied even more suggestive details. The scent of him—leather and musky after-shave—drifted around her, the warmth of his body a welcome heat on a summer night that had cooled surprisingly fast after sundown. Searching for a fraction of space, she shifted in the saddle as they galloped through trees. Her movement elicited a sharp intake of breath behind her.

It was the first indication Brock might be feeling some of the wayward attraction, too. She wanted to turn around to face him, to see the expression on his face, but his palm was a firm weight against her belly, his fingers a light graze of warmth along the inside of her hip. The barrier of her leggings didn't begin to dull the intimacy of the sensation.

She didn't know how she'd walk away from him at the end of this ride. For that matter, she didn't know how she'd look him in the eye again after this. It was all so very…

Sensual.

Her heart pounded faster than the horse's hooves. She told herself it was because of the incredible stress she'd been under. The frustrated tension of seeing her sister suffer and not being able to help. The unbearable strain of working with a man she despised in order to find evidence of his misdeeds.

All that anxiety had shoved her to a breaking point, leaving her with zero reserves now, when tempted with the heady pleasure of a generous, honorable man's touch. Brock had strode into her world, putting the bully Ventura in his place, and Hannah had been intrigued. Curious. Attracted.

Now, adding to that attraction, the horseback ride tantalized her with needs she normally shoved to the backburner. These were desires she'd ignored easily enough in the past, only indulging them within committed relationships.

Brock's touch teased her with all the ways she'd gone unfulfilled. Because no man had ever ignited the sort of awareness she felt tonight. As if the slightest increase in pressure from his hands would unleash a tide of passion and desire that would completely sweep her away.

Then, suddenly, her cabin was in sight, the tiny pinprick of light from an upstairs window growing as they neared the small structure. She focused on it like a beacon in a dark sea, telling herself this churn of sensual thought would recede once she arrived there.

When Brock leaned back slightly in the saddle, drawing the horse to a halt, Hannah waited for a break in the seductive spell. But even as Brock swung a leg over the saddle and jumped down to the ground, her nerve endings still danced with awareness. Anticipation.

Glancing at him, she met his gaze for a moment, and that only worsened the heat. He reached up to help her dismount, his hands ready to assist her. And she simply fell into his arms. No thought. No planning. She slid down, her body against his in a way that set her on fire. Then she was reaching for him, wrapping her arms around his neck.

Kissing him.

His lips sealed to hers, his arms banding around her back and waist. She dangled in midair for a moment against him, her breasts pressed to the hard wall of his chest. Flames licked over her skin as their mouths fused, tongues tangling. A mindless need roared through her, a hunger to have more of this. More of him.

When he set her on her feet, he edged back to look at her, his breath coming fast.

She knew it was wise of him to separate them. To break the mesmerizing contact. To give them a moment to think about this. But there in the endless dark, with only the horse and the wind as her witnesses, she couldn't scavenge any reason to deny herself this heat. This connection. This kind of intense pleasure she'd never experienced before. Perhaps it was the inky blackness of the night that made it feel surreal, like a dream she didn't want to wake up from.

All Hannah knew was that her body went to his like a magnet drawn to a more powerful one.

A raw sound rose up in his throat as she found his lips and kissed him again. Brock wrapped his hands around her, this time with more intent and purpose. She could feel the difference in how he flexed his fingers against her, the added pressure tantalizing her all the more.

"Hannah." He breathed her name against her mouth. "Are you sure?"

"Positive." She gripped his biceps, wanting him inside where she could take his clothes off.

Straightening, she withdrew the keycard for the door from the small hip pocket sewn into her leggings. Her fingers were unsteady as she slid it through the reader.

"I don't have protection with me, but my house is just through the woods."

"I have something." An old habit inspired by a college friend's pregnancy. A good thing, because she wasn't willing to wait for him to make a trip to his place.

As she pushed open the door, she knew stepping over the threshold was a point of no return. But she had no reservations about this. It was a moment of pleasure in a year of hell. The only things she felt now were hunger and need, the desire for him so stark she couldn't begin to account for it. Her gaze met his in the dim light cast by two cast-iron sconces that flanked the stone fireplace mantel.

Extending her hand to him, she threaded her fingers through his. "Please. Come in."

Something had happened on that shared horseback ride.

A switch had been thrown. A blaze had started, and there was no putting it out now.

Brock told himself he'd given her every out. Every

option of changing her mind. And she'd refused. He couldn't fight himself and her, too. Not when he'd wanted her from the first moment he'd seen her. Not when the stress of being a McNeill was at an all-time high. He felt like the whole damn world around him was poised to collapse when the blackmailer went public.

How could he refuse a night to forget about that, just for a little while, and lose himself in the promise of what Hannah was offering?

So, stepping into her two-bedroom cabin, he closed and locked the door behind him. Gave himself a moment to try to muster some scrap of restraint, if only to ensure they made it to a bed instead of tearing off their clothes in the middle of the living area.

But Hannah was having none of it. With the same certainty she'd shown when she slid off his horse and into his arms, she came to him now. She wrapped her arms around his neck, pressed herself into him. This time, he didn't hold back, allowing the full impact of those sweetly feminine curves to work their seductive magic.

Purely potent. Totally intoxicating.

The chemistry was intense, the heat so strong he thought they might combust right there. He cupped her cheek, angling her chin higher to taste her more thoroughly. She tipped off his Stetson, winging it to an empty ladder-back chair near the door. Her ball cap had already fallen away, her silky blond waves tickling his arm, teasing along his skin.

He walked her backward, toward the dark hallway where the bedrooms were. He'd helped build this place with his brothers long ago—now it was a guest residence for visitors. Hannah let herself be led, moving with him, pausing near the kitchen bar long enough to pluck a leather handbag from the counter. She brought it with them into the darkened bedroom.

He flicked the switch by the door that lit a small gas fireplace on one wall opposite the bed, the low flames the only light in the room as he toed the door closed behind them. Hannah had already peeled off her shirt, and the sight of her creamy skin, breasts cradled in blue lace, nearly undid him.

Pulse thrumming hard, he reached for her, needing his hands on her. Her skin was incredibly soft as he drew her to him, the scent of her—something sweet and heady like orange blossoms—making him desperate to taste her. He kissed his way down her neck, searching for the source of the scent, taking his time on the journey to lick along her collarbone, nip her shoulder and ear.

She gripped the hem of his T-shirt and hauled it up his back and over his head. The pace was too fast but the hunger too keen to slow down as they undressed each other, tasting and touching as they unveiled themselves. Her creamy skin was rosy in the firelight, her hair turning from platinum to strawberry blond as it fell along her shoulder. He slid a finger beneath one bra strap, tugging it off, tracing the scalloped edge of lace before the fabric fell away.

She arched into him, the taut, pebbled peaks of her breasts almost close enough to taste. Bending to take her in his mouth, he circled the tip of one and then the other, unfastening the hook to free her and cupping the soft weights in his hands. Her moan was a sexy siren's song in his ear.

"Please, please, please," she chanted, one hand on his belt, a fingertip tracing the top edge of the leather.

Grazing his abs. Making him impossibly harder.

Torching all restraint.

She took a condom packet from her purse and put it on the bed. He eyed it before helping her with the belt. Quickly his pants were gone, his boots were gone, boxers gone.

His undressing was faster than hers, since she tangled her feet in the leggings while she watched him disrobe, her attention so damn flattering.

Brock lifted her in his arms, skimming off the scrap of blue lace around her hips before he pulled her down to the white duvet with him. She made soft, sexy sounds of approval in his ear as she speared her fingers into his hair and drew him down to kiss her. Shadows flickered across the bed beside them in the firelight, the need for her—for this—ratcheting higher.

He'd never bedded a woman so fast. Never imagined a night like this where desire smoked away reason and sensual hunger roared with predatory demand. But Hannah was right there with him, her hands shifting lower to smooth down his chest, back up his arms. All the while she urged him faster, whispering soft commands to touch her. Taste her.

He couldn't get enough of her.

When she placed the condom packet in his hands, he tore it open like a man who'd been deprived for years. He wanted to take his time. See the way she looked when pleasure overtook her.

But this thing—whatever it was between them—was beyond that. It was a fever in the blood, driving hotter and faster with every breath.

Rolling the condom into place, he met her gaze. Her gray eyes watched him, her lips parted as her breath came in fast pants. He captured her mouth, kissing her as he positioned himself between her thighs. Edged his way inside.

He caught her cry of pleasure before she arched her neck and back. Her nails dug into his shoulders, and her body went still at last. When he started to move, he took his time, building the pleasure while she adjusted to him. Her foot pinned his calf for a moment, then slid higher, an ankle hooking around his waist. He gripped her thigh and angled her body. Nearly died of how damn good she felt.

Brock waited, trying like hell to slow down. To temper the need. But then, Hannah breathed in his ear, nipping the lobe and licking his neck just beneath it. Somehow that pushed things higher, and started the banked tension building again. He reached between them to touch her, teasing out the pleasure for her, too.

He could feel that same tension in her. Her head tossed from side to side, the rest of her going still. He kissed her again, taking her lips just as the sweet squeeze of her release gripped him tight.

The spasms went on and on, nudging him over the edge and into oblivion. His shout mingled with her soft cries, a chorus of the most perfect pleasure he'd ever felt.

With a woman he barely knew.

The realization slammed home just as he caught his breath. Just as some form of reason returned. Still, the fact that they didn't know each other well didn't take anything away from whatever they'd just experienced. It had been powerful. Passionate.

Incredibly fulfilling even as it made him want her all over again.

In other words, it was pure insanity.

Brock sank into the mattress beside her, rolling her to his side so they lay together before he drew half of the duvet over their bare bodies.

"That was the craziest thing I've ever done." Her words were softened by the wonder in her voice. The amazement. A hint of a smile curved her lips. "I don't even know your last name."

A stir of warning prickled along his shoulders. He'd withheld it on purpose, of course. But it didn't matter now. She certainly hadn't been trying to get close to him because he was a McNeill. That much had been established.

Besides, as an actress, she had her own path to fame and fortune.

"McNeill." He glanced over at her, smoothing a long blond wave away from her cheek. "Brock McNeill."

Something shifted in her eyes. A recognition, yes. But not the speculative, almost greedy kind that he'd sometimes seen over the years.

No. He could have sworn Hannah Ryder all but recoiled. There was the slightest flinch. A fractional crinkle of her smooth brow. A stillness.

As if the name meant something to her, and not in a good way.

He wanted to ask her about it. Or at least, to talk to her and make some sense of what just happened. But she was already sliding away from him.

"I'm so sorry." She shook her head. "And embarrassed. But I just remembered I have an early call on set tomorrow." She slipped out from under the duvet, turning to plant her feet on the floor. "I don't know what I was thinking. But I guess that's the whole point. I wasn't really thinking."

Perhaps her reaction didn't have anything to do with his name. Maybe she was just feeling the bite of morning-after regret—far too soon. That much, he could understand. The attraction had caught them like a tornado, touching down with fevered intensity.

He put a hand on her shoulder. "I'll go in a minute," he assured her. "Is everything okay? Are you all right?"

"I'm fine." She nodded, not making eye contact. "I'm just… This is completely awkward, right?" Hopping to her feet, she found her shirt and slid it over her head, the dark T-shirt covering her to the tops of her thighs. "Would you mind if we talked tomorrow, when I've got my head on straight again?"

Something was off here. Wrong.

He was missing it, but he wasn't sure what he could accomplish by staying any longer when she was clearly agitated. He understood that. And she wasn't the only one feeling rattled by what just happened. He just wished he could be sure that the only thing upsetting her was how fast things had escalated between them, and not something connected to his family name. The McNeills already had enough trouble brewing.

"Of course." Nodding, he scooped his clothes off the floor and started to dress. "I'll come by the set tomorrow and we'll talk then."

She opened her mouth, then snapped it shut again. Nodding, she pulled an afghan off the end of the bed and wrapped it around herself.

"Sure." She hugged the blanket tighter while he finished dressing. "And, um, thank you for the ride home."

He couldn't help a wry chuckle as he stepped into his boots. "I sure as hell hope the ride isn't what you remember most about this night." Leaning close to her, he brushed a kiss over her cheek, wanting nothing more than to remind her that what just happened hadn't been a fluke. But he understood about early wake-up calls. "We'll definitely be talking more tomorrow. Good night, Hannah."

Striding out of the bedroom, he retrieved his hat off the chair and dropped it on his head before stepping into the night. If Hannah was hiding something from him—if she had something against the McNeills—he had every intention of finding out.

Three

Hannah knew she couldn't hide from Brock Mc-Neill, but she was tempted to try the next day when he hadn't made an appearance on the set by mid-morning. How could the hottest night of her life have gone so terribly wrong?

The sexy rancher who'd turned her inside out was a *McNeill*.

Seated in a makeup chair under a canvas tent erected near the barn where she'd been shooting earlier, Hannah tried unsuccessfully to read through a script to take her mind off of Brock. She tried to get comfortable. There was a full-length mirror in front of her, and a cup of coffee stuffed in the mesh drink holder of her chair. Dressed in her period costume—a calico dress complete with petticoats and chemise—Hannah scrolled through the script for a space Western on her phone. It didn't take a genius to know she was starting to get typecast as a ditz—a role she'd done well once and should have distanced herself from afterward. She played something similar in *Winning the West*, but she would have taken a role as an extra if it meant getting to work on an Antonio Ventura set. Shoving aside her phone, she wished she could feel outrage about her career. Instead, all she felt was anger at herself for making a selfish decision last night.

How could she have indulged herself that way, putting her own needs before her mission? It had never occurred to her that the casually dressed rancher who personally oversaw his horses could be a member of one of the nation's wealthiest families. Hannah knew all about the connection between Cheyenne's ranching McNeills and the Manhattan branch of the family and their lucrative resort chain. She'd also read up on the ties between the Silicon Valley start-up, Transparent, principally owned by Damon McNeill and his brothers.

Hannah had researched all of them carefully before she accepted the film role on McNeill land because of the secret connection between the Ventura family and the McNeills. A connection they'd all hidden so thoroughly, she wasn't sure how many people even knew about it besides her. Not that Hannah cared about the secrets and scandals of the rich. She'd simply done her homework to find out if the Mc-Neills were potential allies or enemies in her quest for justice for her sister.

And despite all the research she'd completed—even briefly working for the Ventura family's cleaning service—she still couldn't be certain. It could go either way. Certainly, Brock McNeill had shown no liking for Antonio. They'd behaved as though they were strangers when they spoke on the set yesterday—one more reason why Hannah would have never taken Brock for one of the McNeill family.

Restless and uneasy, Hannah shot from the chair to pace the temporary makeup and dressing area. She hadn't gone three steps when Callie raced into the tent, her work apron covered with pins and her usually sleek ponytail twisted into a haphazard knot.

"There you are!" The wardrobe assistant skidded to a stop, one sandal catching on the tassels of a floor mat. Her cheeks were pink with hectic color. "Hannah, you have a visitor on set." She lifted her dark eyebrows and lowered her voice. "The hot cowboy from yesterday."

Tension squeezed Hannah's shoulders even as warmth stirred in her belly. How could she pretend the same ease with him that she had yesterday, knowing his identity? Knowing the McNeills hid a connection to Antonio Ventura, the man she hated beyond reason? Not even Meryl Streep could pull off that kind of acting job.

"He's here?" Hannah asked finally. Stalling.

She peered into the full-length mirror, wondering if her expression revealed her distress.

Callie stepped closer, looking at Hannah's face in the mirror. "He said you were expecting him. What's wrong?"

"Nothing. Just a little nervous, I guess." She forced a smile, needing to get it together before she saw Brock. If only she understood his family's link to the Venturas.

Was there a chance her relationship with Brock could help her learn something useful about Antonio? Something that would aid her efforts to unmask him for the monster he was?

Steeling herself for the performance she needed to give for the sake of her sister, Hannah hoped she could extricate herself from an intimate relationship without alienating Brock altogether. Because while she was willing to leverage a friendship to learn anything she could about Antonio, she drew the line at allowing Brock back into her bed ever again now that she knew he was a McNeill.

The rest of the world might not know the truth about the Ventura and McNeill connection, but Hannah had unearthed the secret from a coworker at the Venturas' cleaning service.

Paige McNeill, Brock's stepmother, had married Brock's father under an assumed name. She was actually the missing Hollywood heiress Eden Harris. Daughter of the actress Barbara Harris and director Emilio Ventura. Stepsister to Antonio Ventura himself.

So until Hannah knew where the McNeills stood on the issue of the family they had never publicly acknowledged, maybe it was best to treat all of them—Brock included—like they were her potential enemies.

Brock knew he should stay away from Hannah Ryder.

Publicly, it made sense to keep the relationship quiet since he didn't need to draw more attention to his family in the days—hours, perhaps—before a scandal broke. And privately, Brock had yet to figure out the expression on Hannah's face when she'd learned of his identity last night, so it wasn't a good idea to get too involved with a woman so clearly rattled by the McNeill name.

Yet here he was on the set of her film before noon the day after they'd met. After they'd parted awkwardly and she'd dominated his thoughts all night.

He paced behind the camera while the set crew worked to change some components in front of the lens. Lights were rolled out of the open barn doors and new lights were rolled in on handcarts and dollies. Props were switched. Hay was raked and "fluffed" using methods that rendered it unusable for horses—glue, silicon spray and filler were mixed in to make the piles look bigger against the walls. The whole place bustled with activity while the actors and director were on break.

Brock had missed seeing Hannah's scene earlier in the day, but he'd been busy with his family. His brother Carson's new girlfriend—Emma Layton, a stunt woman for *Winning the West*—had shared what might be an important clue about a connection between the McNeills and the Venturas, one the black-mailer could be exploiting. Emma's mother, Jane, had been hinting at the connection in recent phone conversations. Jane Layton had worked as a maid for the Ventura families for years and had been privy to many of the family's private affairs, but Emma also confided that her mother was emotionally unstable.

So could they trust any information gleaned from Jane Layton?

The McNeill family's private investigator couldn't follow up all the blackmail leads fast enough now that the time had almost expired on the threat to expose Paige McNeill's past. Brock's father was scared his wife was going to have a nervous breakdown, since she hadn't yet fully recovered from her time spent in a coma. And Scarlett, Paige's youngest daughter, refused to speak to any of them while she nursed her anger that they'd somehow forsaken Paige by not trying to work something out with the blackmailer.

Now this.

The woman who'd so thoroughly captivated Brock last night was hiding something, and he was deter-mined to find out what. The family suspected the blackmailer might be working on the film or have a close connection to someone who did. Could Hannah Ryder be capable of blackmail? Anger flared at the thought she might have used sex to get closer to him. He was certain the attraction was real, but the possibility of deception rankled.

He was so caught up in those dark thoughts he didn't hear anyone approach him as he held the side door open for a woman pushing a catering cart of fruit, breakfast pastries and coffee.

"Brock."

The sound of Hannah's voice behind him sent a spike of unwanted heat up his spine. He really needed to get his attraction to her under control until he figured out where she stood in this mess with his family.

Pivoting on his boot heel, he faced her.

She was even lovelier than he remembered. Her hair was pinned up on either side, the back falling in curls that struck him as a vaguely historical style—maybe because the curls were so carefully molded. She wore a frontier-woman kind of gown, too. It was cream-colored and dotted with tiny flowers. The bodice shaped her torso in an exaggerated manner that looked sort of painful—cinching her waist and lifting her breasts in a way guaranteed to draw the eye. The full skirt of her dress would have reached the floor if she didn't have the fabric tucked into the waist, probably to keep it clean when she wasn't filming.

Even her black lace-up boots with tiny heels were from another era.

He battled the urge to touch her. To greet her with a kiss, or a whispered word about how beautiful she looked. Instead, he needed to come straight to the point. He was running out of time to help his family. He needed to know why his name had upset this West Coast actress who shouldn't care about his identity one way or the other.

"Hello, Hannah." His nod was as terse as his tone, but it couldn't be helped. "We said we'd talk more today. Can we go somewhere to speak privately?"

"My next scene is supposed to start filming soon." She seemed different. More guarded.

Which was to be expected, he supposed, even if she didn't have anything to do with the blackmail scheme. He ground his teeth against the frustration of the past few weeks. He was a horse breeder and trainer, damn it. Not a sleuth.

"I need to ask you about last night," he pressed, unwilling to let it go. He simply lowered his voice more and drew her into a dark corner of the barn, between the side door and the open front doors. "About the way you reacted when I told you my name."

There it was.

A tiny flinch. A slight flare of her nostrils.

He'd been with a woman who kept secrets before. He recognized the signs, and it was an experience he refused to repeat.

"I don't know what you mean," she lied smoothly

enough, but the words didn't erase that moment of honest response he'd seen on her face.

"Yes, you do." He wasn't going to drop it. And he wasn't going to let her off the hook. "My family is going through hell right now, Hannah, and if you know something about that—about the threats leveled against the McNeills—"

"I have no idea what you're talking about." She shook her head, the curls brushing her shoulders, catching on the lace detail of her sleeve. Her face paled. "What threats?"

Behind him, another dolly rumbled past with electronic equipment, but with the shouting and noise made by the crew, he wasn't worried about being overheard.

He plowed ahead. "Someone has been threatening my family. Time is running out for me to figure out who's behind those threats." He stepped closer to her, sensing movement behind him as the set workers adjusted lights overhead. "We're being blackmailed—"

His speech wavered, then halted, as something heavy cracked the back of his skull. He had a flash of awareness that he was falling. A moment to see panic on Hannah's lovely face before...

The world went black.

"Brock!" Hannah watched in horror as the big, strong man beside her crumpled to the ground.

It took her a moment to process what had happened. One of the overhead lights had broken free of the grid, hitting the back of Brock's head. The light lay smashed on the floor behind him, the heavy black housing bent on one side. Already, people were shouting, grips and gaffers scrambling to secure the grid and clear the set.

"Brock?" Hannah sank to her knees beside the fallen rancher, her fingers tentative as she touched his shoulder, fear icing her insides. "Are you all right?"

He was breathing, but he remained stone-still.

Two production assistants were suddenly beside her, leaning over him, informing her not to move him.

Because she was flustered and scared, it took her a moment to process why. He had a head injury. He could have a concussion or much worse. A spinal injury would be...

Oh, God. She laid her hand over his, taking his fingers—careful not to move his arm—and squeezing them gently.

"Call 911!" she shouted, even as one of the wardrobe assistants flashed a thumbs-up sign as she spoke into her phone.

Someone was already taking care of that.

The minutes stretched out endlessly as they waited for an ambulance. In the background, Hannah heard the second director yelling at the production staff while someone swept up broken glass. Hannah debated how to reach Brock's family to let someone know what had happened, but she couldn't seem to let go of his hand.

He'd told her someone was threatening his rela-

tives. Blackmailing them. He'd been upset about it—
to the point there was even suspicion of her in his
eyes—before that light had hit him. Did he suspect
her of blackmail?

The thought chilled her even more.

Had he told his family about them? About his
night with her or the way she'd reacted when he mentioned the McNeill name? What if they blamed her
for the accident?

None of it should matter now when Brock was
hurt. But she couldn't afford to get caught up in a
scandal that had nothing to do with her. Brock might
suspect her of something, but she knew she wasn't a
blackmailer. She only wanted evidence against Antonio Ventura, but she couldn't possibly share her
secret agenda with his family. Not even to clear her
name, if it came down to that.

In the distance, she heard the wail of a siren. The
ambulance was getting closer.

Relieved that help was on the way, she let one of
the director's assistants know that she was going to
follow the ambulance to the hospital. Because no
matter how awkward things had gotten between her
and Brock, this was still the man who had kissed her
senseless the night before. The man who'd publicly
told off Antonio.

She needed to be there for him until someone
from his family arrived.

"You're going to be fine," she assured him even
though he couldn't hear her. She stroked her free

hand over the subtle bristle of his jaw. "The ambulance is almost here."

The siren grew louder. Nearby, the production team cleared a path between the doors and Brock, moving aside equipment.

Hannah told herself she should step back out of the way, too. But before she could, she felt Brock stirring.

Relief rushed through her.

"He's waking up!" she shouted to no one in particular, her eyes remaining on him. "He's coming out of it."

She squeezed his hand tighter, watched as he lifted his head ever so slightly. Then, as if he found it too heavy, he rested his head back on the ground, but blinked his eyes open and stared up at her.

"Are you okay?" she asked him, tilting her head to meet his gaze. "It's probably better if you don't move just yet."

She searched his face, looking for clues to any sign of discomfort or injury. Needing him to be okay.

Brock frowned, a scowl wrinkling his forehead as he studied her. When he spoke, his voice was gravelly and deep, his tone oddly distant.

"Who are you?" he asked, his blue eyes never wavering from her face. "Do I know you?"

Four

Was he serious?

Vaguely, she became aware of movement around her, the EMS crew laying a stretcher next to him before gently shuffling her aside to assess Brock's condition.

Did Brock really not remember her?

She squeezed her temples, trying to figure out what that meant. Because while she'd started this day wishing she could have a chance at a do-over with Brock, she had never wanted him to be hurt.

Tension balled tight in her stomach as the EMS workers took his vitals and asked him questions, gathering information about the blow to his head. Hannah paced circles nearby, willing herself to think. To figure out what it meant that Brock didn't recognize her.

He'd stared at her as if she was a total stranger. As if they hadn't been naked together less than twenty-four hours ago.

Her gaze skittered toward him, her heart rate jumping at the sight of him. She couldn't imagine forgetting their time together. Forgetting him. She watched as he tried to wave off the woman taking his blood pressure. Brock reached for his phone, insisting he would call his own physician.

A good sign, right? Except his movements seemed a bit stilted. And when the other EMS worker asked him what day it was, Brock seemed confused.

Worry twisted inside Hannah. For a moment, she considered walking away, before his memory returned. No one would be the wiser that she'd bailed on him.

Except she wasn't that kind of woman. Besides, she should stay close to Brock in case he knew more about Antonio Ventura. Hannah's mission to help her sister came first.

If Brock had forgotten about his night with Hannah, maybe she didn't need to remind him of how far things had gone between them. She could have her chance at a do-over, only this time, she'd be his friend and not his lover.

There would be no expectation of more. No suspicions about why she'd backed away from a relationship so fast. And if a little voice inside her head warned her that it wasn't going to be easy to pretend she wasn't attracted to him?

She'd simply have to ignore it, along with the man's red-hot appeal.

Brock just lay in a hospital bed, skull throbbing, hypoallergenic pillowcase crinkling as he shifted. Some of the pain he attributed to the knot on the back of his head. But the bigger ache came from not knowing how he landed in Cheyenne Regional Medical Center.

There'd been other times in the past he'd woken up to an EMS worker hovering over him. During his rodeo years, he'd broken enough bones and taken enough blows to the head that ER trips had been regular occurrences.

But in the past, he always remembered the fall.

Today? He didn't have a clue what had happened to him. And it didn't take a medical genius to know something was really wrong, considering all the docs who'd come through his exam room to ask him questions and frown over his chart. Where was his family? Not that he expected his older brothers to come running when he fell off a bull. Or his father either, for that matter. But his half sisters normally showed up for him. Maisie, Madeline and Scarlett had always been good to him.

This time, Maisie and Madeline had both texted him their regrets that they couldn't be there because they needed to be by their mother's side before "the scandal broke." Whatever that meant. Scarlett's response was even more puzzling, since she said Cheyenne was too far to drive, but she hoped he felt better soon.

Where in the hell was his youngest sister if not in Cheyenne? He wanted to look back over his texting history—to see if he could make sense of his world again, but he was having the damnedest time operating the cell phone, which was a different model than he remembered.

He stabbed at the touch screen, wondering where the home button had disappeared to.

The door to his room opened and one of his attending physicians entered—a tall, genial guy with a thick Eastern European accent. Brock slid his phone onto the bedside table, anxious to be released so he could get home and wait for his head to clear. The whole world felt off-kilter, but if there was some kind of scandal brewing that could hurt his family, Brock needed to be with his brothers and sisters, not sitting in a hospital bed.

Brock straightened, sliding his feet to the floor.

"Whoa, Mr. McNeill." Dr. Kreshnik hurried closer, his clipboard clattering to the tile as he reached for Brock's arm to steady him. "You've had head trauma. We don't want you moving too quickly on your own."

"I'm fine," Brock protested, knowing he would feel better at home. "I don't know who decided I needed the ER visit, but I'm definitely ready to be discharged."

"I'm afraid that's not possible, Mr. McNeill." The physician frowned as he retrieved the chart from the floor. "We want to evaluate you further."

"I've been here for five hours." Time might be fuzzy for him, but he'd messaged his sisters from the ambulance so he knew he'd been at the hospital that long. The room spun a bit, but then stopped. He was still wearing his street clothes and they'd already done a CT scan. He could have the results sent to his specialist.

"You're exhibiting signs of amnesia…" The doctor continued speaking, rattling off words like "short-term episode" and "more tests."

But Brock's brain stuck on that word. *Amnesia.*

Was that why he couldn't recall what was going on in his family? Why he didn't remember the accident that brought him in here? But he knew his own name. Could remember his friends. His family.

His head throbbed harder.

While the medical expert spouted something about care plans, a soft knock sounded on the exam room door. One of his sisters, maybe?

"Come in," Brock called, needing an ally to bust him out of the facility.

But the woman who stepped into the room juggling two steaming foam cups wasn't a sister. And he thanked his lucky stars for that.

Her generous curves and platinum waves were

the stuff fantasies were made of, although her outfit made her look like she'd just stepped off the prairie. Her long, flower-dotted skirt was something from another era and modest in the extreme. But the shirt she wore with it was another matter altogether, the stiff fabric as tight as a corset, nipping her waist and drawing the eye upward to her breasts.

No amount of head trauma would have kept him from noticing her. From feeling the spark of attraction.

"I can come back," she offered, hesitating just inside the door when she spotted the man in scrubs and a lab coat next to Brock's bed. "Is this a bad time?"

"Come in," Brock insisted, waving her forward even though he had no idea who she was. He had a vague memory of her sitting beside him when he first regained consciousness, an unreadable expression in her beautiful gray eyes. But before that—nothing.

Who was she?

"Ms. Ryder." Dr. Kreshnik nodded at the mystery woman. "Any luck getting in touch with his family?"

"I'm afraid not." She shook her head, the curls bouncing lightly as she moved toward Brock and passed him one of the foam cups. He noticed there was no wedding ring on her finger. "I left a message with the foreman at the Creek Spill Ranch, however, and he promised to contact Brock's brothers personally."

That was the last thing Brock needed. He'd spent a lifetime flying under the radar of his big family, and with good reason. He had no desire to be in the McNeill spotlight, especially when it sounded like his family was in crisis.

"That won't be necessary," Brock interjected. "I'll sign whatever you need to release me." The sooner he got back home, the sooner his head would stop pounding. The sooner he could figure out what was going on with his family. The fact that none of them was here with him spoke volumes.

Dr. Kreshnik frowned while Brock sipped the coffee—too sweet for his taste, but still good.

"You've had a head injury—" The doctor looked like he was winding up for a long diatribe, his pen stabbing into the top paper on the clipboard he carried.

"And I need to rest, not have more tests." Concussions could affect short-term memory. And he knew concussion protocol by heart. No doubt his head would clear in a few days. "So if you want to write up any medical recommendations you have for me, I'll be on my way. My family needs me at home." Brock turned to the woman while the doctor pivoted on his heel and called for one of the nurses. "Is your vehicle here?"

Her coffee cup froze midway to her lips; she appeared surprised to be a part of the conversation. He noticed a name—Hannah—had been written in gold marker on the front of her take-out beverage.

"Sure. Um. Yes." She lowered her drink, standing straighter. "I borrowed one of the set vehicles to follow the ambulance."

Set vehicles?

He didn't have a clue what that meant, but he remembered she had been beside him when he regained consciousness. Everything else—including what he'd been doing with her—was hazy.

"Great. If you don't mind dropping me off at the Creek Spill, I can meet you downstairs in ten minutes." He knew the hospital couldn't keep him here against his will.

Her gray eyes darted from him to the doctor and back again, but she nodded. She reached inside her handbag for a set of keys and slipped out the door.

There was something peculiar about her that went beyond her odd outfit. Something in those uneasy gray eyes of hers, but maybe it was simply worry for him.

Right now, she was his fastest ticket home so he could figure out what was going on with his family. Besides, she'd be able to provide some answers about the accident that had landed him here.

Assuming, of course, he could trust her.

Short-term retrograde amnesia.

Hannah mulled over the term as she steered the compact car onto the county route on their way back to the Creek Spill Ranch half an hour later. The orderly who had accompanied Brock outside had handed her the discharge papers with instructions for follow-up care, giving Hannah a moment to see the diagnosis while Brock buckled his seat belt for the ride. Now, chewing her lip between answering the questions Brock fired her way, she wondered what exactly the amnesia would mean for him.

Did "short-term" imply the problem was temporary? Or had he lost only his short-term memories? She couldn't even ask Brock since he was clearly still reeling from the injury. He'd asked *her* how the accident happened, why she was dressed like a frontier woman, why a movie scene was being filmed on his land and how long they'd known one another.

She was honest about how they met, and even admitted he'd given her a ride home the night before. She just skated over the part about throwing herself into his arms afterward, seizing the chance to conceal their intimate connection.

But she found it surprising that he'd forgotten her yet knew that his family needed him now. He'd said as much to Dr. Kreshnik, but it hardly seemed possible he would recall the McNeills were being blackmailed if he had amnesia. Then again, maybe he'd put things together from reading texts on his phone. She knew he'd been receiving messages from his siblings. No wonder he'd been able to verify today's date when one of the doctors had asked him about it, even though that very same question had confused him in the ambulance. Brock must have been able to orient himself with the evidence on his screen.

"Honestly, Brock, are you really sure you want me to take you home? I couldn't help but notice those discharge papers." She removed one hand from the steering wheel to point at the paperwork now resting on the console between them. "If the doctor is correct that you have amnesia—"

"I've hit my head before. Bull riding." He stretched his legs in the cramped quarters, one denim-clad knee bumping the dashboard. "I know concussion symptoms and I have a good neurologist in Denver. I'll give his office a call when I get home."

She bit her lip, unsure how much to argue. A concussion could make someone irritable. Act out of character. She'd read that much online when she'd been in the waiting room today, hoping all the while someone from his family would come take her place. No one had. But at least she'd learned a little more about head injuries, and she knew that stress could aggravate his symptoms.

"That's a good idea." She tried being agreeable as she turned off the county route onto the private road that led to Creek Spill. "But I'm not sure a concussion alone can account for how much time you've lost if you don't remember that there's a movie being filmed on your land."

Winning the West had been on-site for almost two weeks, and before that, the location scout had been staying with Brock's older brother, Cody, while she worked out the logistics for the filming.

"I'll look into it once I check on my family." He rapped his knuckles lightly on the inside of the window. Anxious? Impatient? Or maybe just agitated. "And keep going past the main house. My family will be at my father's place. I could tell from my sisters' messages today that something is really wrong at home."

The obvious worry in his voice struck a chord with her. Hannah understood all too well the way fierce family loyalty could drive a person to great lengths and behave in a way they wouldn't normally. Like checking themselves out of a hospital when they needed medical care. Or taking a job working for a man who'd molested a family member.

They had more in common than she'd realized.

"I might know something about that," she admitted, wanting to help him if only to make up for the way she'd omitted details about their relationship. "You mentioned something to me about your family before that light hit you."

She drove past the main house at Creek Spill Ranch, as he'd asked. She hoped he remembered the directions to his father's home since she didn't know where she was headed any longer.

"Tell me," he said simply, turning the focus of those blue eyes on her. "What exactly did I say?"

She shivered with awareness, feeling the impact of his gaze even as she kept her attention on the road ahead. Memories of being with him tantalized her. Taunted her with all she'd never experience again.

"I—" Her voice hitched on a breathless note. She cleared her throat and tried not to think about the way he'd touched her. "That is, you mentioned your family had been going through hell lately. That someone was threatening the McNeills."

"I knew something was wrong when no one came to the hospital." His fingers tightened into a fist, his shoulders tensing. "Threatening how?"

She hated to upset him when he was in this condition. But he had the right to know. "Blackmail."

He bit off a curse and reached to withdraw his phone from his back pocket. "There's got to be some clue about what's going on in here. My sister mentioned a scandal, but I'll be damned if I know what she's talking about." He stabbed at the screen, his movements agitated as he muttered, "This thing must be new."

Did the scandal have anything to do with the secret she knew? Her skin prickled, a guilty feeling pinching her conscience that she might know more about Brock's family than he did. But had he forgotten the truth only because of the amnesia? Or had his family carefully hidden their connection to the Venturas?

The road grew narrower as Hannah drove deeper into the woods. Lost in more ways than one, Hannah wondered how she'd gotten herself so deeply embroiled in Brock's life so quickly.

"Am I still going the right way?" she asked.

He glanced up just as his phone chimed. "Yes. My father's place is up here on the right. Just around that bend."

When he glanced back down at his screen, he

asked her for her phone number in case he needed to contact her later. She gave it to him, wondering if he would be in touch with her again, or if it was just a formality. Moments later, he sucked in a sharp breath.

"What is it?" She slowed down as she guided the car around the corner.

Brock's attention remained on the phone. His voice—when he spoke—sounded hollow. "A Hollywood tabloid just put my stepmother's name in the headlines."

Foreboding squeezed her belly. She took her eyes off the road long enough to see his expression.

The shock in his voice sounded genuine when he spoke again.

"Apparently my father's wife is Hollywood royalty." He peered over at her and Hannah hurried to return her focus to the road, afraid her face might reveal her lack of surprise.

She swallowed hard, pretending a confusion she didn't feel. "What do you mean?"

"If this report can be believed, Paige Samara Mc-Neill is actually Eden Harris, the daughter of Emilio Ventura and B-movie actress Barbara Harris."

Hannah waited the space of a heartbeat. And then another.

"That means your stepmother is my director Antonio's stepsister." She hated even saying the bastard's name. But she needed to ask Brock the question that mattered the most to her. "Did you know about that?"

Brock shook his head. "You mean half sister," he said absently, his gaze on the log cabin home ahead of them with several vehicles parked out front. "If this is true, Paige would be Antonio Ventura's half sister."

"Not in a biological sense. Antonio is Emilio's adopted son." Hannah pulled over, parking behind a pickup. She had researched her sister's tormentor thoroughly, but the fact that Antonio was adopted was common knowledge. Emilio Ventura had already been a famous director in his own right before he married Antonio's mother, and he'd made headlines when he adopted his wife's son.

The son had followed in his father's footsteps, acquiring millions along with the Ventura filmmaking connections once Emilio retired. Then, he'd misused the power and prestige to intimidate Hope, banking on her silence. Or that no one would believe her.

"My father's marriage to Paige was never legal since she wed under a fake name." Brock swiped a hand over his face. Rubbed his temples. "My family—my sisters—must be reeling." He held up his phone long enough for her to see the photo on the screen of a teenage Eden Harris next to a photo of Paige's daughters with Donovan McNeill. The resemblance, especially with the youngest daughter, was unmistakable. "Wyoming doesn't recognize common law marriage. So this makes them all illegitimate."

If Hannah had to guess, she would say that

Brock's shock was genuine. That he hadn't known about any connection between the McNeills and the Venturas. But was that because of the amnesia? Or had he truly never known about his stepmother's identity?

Either way, for today, he was clearly stunned.

"I'm so sorry." She reached across the console to lay a hand on his arm, the need to offer comfort too strong to resist even though she knew that touching this man had a powerful effect on her. "Is there anything I can do to help?"

She wished someone from his family would come out to the car to help him inside. Was he steady enough on his feet? But there was no sign of movement in the log cabin home.

Brock's gaze dipped to where she touched him. It shouldn't have set off sparks, especially given the family crisis he was dealing with. Yet, strangely, that's exactly what happened. His blue eyes lifted, locking in on hers.

Her breath caught.

"Are you sure nothing happened last night? After I brought you home?"

Had his memories returned? Was the doctor wrong about the amnesia? Brock had been in the emergency room so briefly.

Visions of their time together spun through her mind so vividly she feared he'd somehow see them in her eyes. But she couldn't afford to get tangled up with a McNeill—especially not now that his connection to the Venturas was public knowledge. What if her unwise affair somehow compromised Hope's position to bring charges against Antonio? Or made other potential victims less inclined to confide in Hannah?

"We just talked." She scavenged a smile as she pulled her hand away from the warmth of his arm. She thumbed the silver ring on her finger, a piece that matched one she'd given to her sister. "That's all."

Her heart thudded from the lie. And the impossible attraction that wouldn't go away.

Brock nodded as he slid the hospital discharge papers off the console. "It just makes me wonder why I sought you out today on the set to tell you about the blackmail." He levered open the door and stepped out onto the lush green grass. "That doesn't seem like something I'd confide to a woman I just met."

She could see his point. But she couldn't think of an answer.

"I don't know." Shrugging, she turned the key in the ignition. "But I hope you feel better soon."

His brusque nod was his only answer before he pivoted on his boot heel and strode up the stone path toward the cabin.

Hannah couldn't help but think about how different their parting had been the night before when she'd been wrapped in nothing but an afghan, and he'd promised they'd talk more soon.

Today, she'd gotten what she wanted—distance

from a McNeill. A do-over on the relationship that should have never happened in the first place.

Yet in the process, she'd made him suspicious of her.

And with a blackmailer on the loose, Hannah wondered if she'd just made a huge mistake.

Five

Scarlett McNeill sped north on Pacific Coast Highway, the car radio tuned into the same news she'd heard on a loop, over and over again, since the family scandal broke.

With an effort, she eased her foot off the accelerator as she crept too close to the car in front of her. Her whole body felt brittle with tension, her brain too stunned to think.

"… Eden Harris, daughter of troubled actress Barbara Harris and famed director Emilio Ventura, has been living under an assumed name for over twenty years." The disembodied voice on the radio reported the story using almost the same exact wording Scarlett had heard on two other stations since she'd slid into the driver's seat of her rented vehicle.

She needed to get to Logan's house. Needed his embrace to ground her when her life felt too surreal. Everything she thought she'd known about her mother was a lie. The woman she called "Mom," a seemingly simple woman who'd shunned the spotlight for Scarlett's entire life, had run away from one of Hollywood's most famous households when she'd been seventeen years old. And she'd never breathed a word of it to anyone.

Worse, Scarlett wasn't in Cheyenne with her sisters or her half brothers when the news broke, she was on her own trying to deal with the fallout. Of course, they'd all known a scandal was brewing after Scarlett had been handed the first blackmail letter by a stranger in an LA nightclub earlier in the month. But while Scarlett had been a proponent of trying to work with the blackmailer or the police to prevent the scandal from hitting the tabloids, her father and siblings had decided not to bargain with an extortionist. Scarlett had been angry and indignant on her mother's behalf, all the more so since Paige was recovering from a coma after a hiking accident and wasn't well enough to fight for herself.

Between that fundamental difference of opinion and her brother hiring a private investigator to keep tabs on her on a trip to LA, Scarlett had it with her family. She'd moved up her timetable to relocate to Hollywood and try her hand at acting. She didn't regret it, but right now, the eight hundred miles between her and Cheyenne might as well have been a million.

Thankfully, she'd arrived at Logan's. His driveway was on the left, and she pulled off Pacific Coast Highway in front of the three-bay garage. While she parked, she continued to listen to the radio broadcaster's story. "Ms. Harris, calling herself Paige Samara, married heir to the McNeill Resorts empire Donovan McNeill, and has three daughters with him. No word yet on whether that marriage would still be legal under the circumstances."

Scarlett switched off the ignition, quieting the broadcaster's voice. The sudden silence didn't stop the last words from echoing around and around her head, though.

She'd just barely renewed her relationship with actor Logan King, but he'd seemed sincere about wanting a second chance with her. About caring for her.

Today, she needed to believe in that, in him. Locking the car behind her, she shoved open the side gate that led to the outdoor stairs alongside Logan's beach house. Running down the steps, she followed the sound of the waves crashing on the rocks below until she emerged on the patio behind the house.

"Logan!" she called, not seeing him right away.

His house opened onto the patio, with a wall of glass doors that almost completely retracted so the living room could be open on one side.

Peering into the open space, she saw him emerge from the kitchen. She had a quick glimpse of his dark hair and green eyes, his strong shoulders. He was already reaching for her.

She dropped her purse on the ground and realized she was shaking as she lifted her arms to slide around him.

"Are you okay?" he asked against her hair, kissing the top of her head. "Do you want to go home and be with your family?" He stroked a hand down her spine, warm and comforting. Enticing, in spite of everything. "I planned to fly to Cheyenne later in the week to film my final scenes in *Winning the West*, but I can change my flight so we can travel together."

She breathed in the scent of his aftershave mingled with the salty air blowing off the waves hitting the beach below them. The rhythm of his heartbeat and the steady crash of the surf helped to ease some of the panic in her chest.

Logan had a prominent role in the movie shooting on the McNeill ranch. He had offered her his beach house while he was out of town since she was staying in a hotel suite in Beverly Hills until she found a place of her own. But she was trying to take it slower with Logan this time after the way she'd thrown herself into their relationship when they'd first met.

"That's kind of you." She eased back to look up at him. The sun was starting to set, bathing the sky in shades of pink and purple. "I haven't been able to think that far ahead. I'm just so…stunned."

He drew her over to one of the love seats that looked out toward the water and tugged her down onto a cushion beside him.

"I will worry about you if you're here by yourself." He held her shoulders as he looked into her eyes. "I know you were upset with your brother that he had a private investigator keeping tabs on you. But if your family is worried that the blackmailer might target you again, then I'm damned well concerned, too."

Her dark hair blew across her cheek as the wind picked up. She peeled a strand away from her lips, touched that Logan would think about her safety.

"The last blackmail note was delivered to Cheyenne, so there is more reason to believe the person threatening the McNeills is now in Wyoming, not LA." She had kept in contact with her sisters throughout the day, aware of how events were unfolding. She might be upset with her family, but she wasn't abandoning them either. "The instructions for depositing funds into an offshore account were sent by email this afternoon, although my family ignored them since they refused to deal with the blackmailer." And now, they would all be paying a different kind of price. "According to the PI firm, the email originated at an internet service provider based in Cheyenne."

Scarlett had given up apartment hunting before noon, unable to concentrate with the texts coming from her sisters.

"How's your mother doing?" Logan asked. "Has she said anything about the scandal?"

"No. I know she's still recovering from her accident, but I can't believe she hasn't said what she thinks about this story, or if it's true." Scarlett's feelings about her mother had been all over the map since learning the news. "I go back and forth between feeling betrayed and wondering if she has a really good reason for hiding the truth about her past."

"I've seen the photos the media have been posting since the story broke. The family resemblance between you and Eden Harris is strong."

"I know." She couldn't deny it. Of her mother's three daughters, Scarlett had always resembled their mother the most, a point of frustration for her since Maisie and Madeline were more traditionally beautiful. But even Scarlett had to admit the old photos of Eden Harris revealed a lovely girl. A different kind of beauty, perhaps. One more suited to the era she'd been raised in.

A random thought occurred to her, one of many racing through her brain as she stared out at the sunset over the water. "I've been worried about getting a break in Hollywood, and as it turns out, my maternal grandfather was once one of the most powerful figures in the film industry."

"And your mother's adopted brother is my director." Logan had no affection for the man in charge of *Winning the West*. He had said more than once he couldn't wait to be done working for Antonio Ventura.

"Do you think Antonio is loathsome enough to blackmail his own sister?" Scarlett knew Antonio had confiscated Logan's cell phone on a shoot in the Congo Republic earlier in the year, in a misguided attempt to help his cast "bond." So she knew he was already regarded as a difficult director.

"I wouldn't put anything past the guy," Logan muttered darkly, slumping back in the seat. "But he sure doesn't need the money. It seems unlikely he'd risk committing a serious crime for a payday when he rakes in an obscene amount for each film he directs."

Scarlett couldn't begin to imagine who was doing this to her family. She leaned back in the love seat, closer to Logan.

"You're right. And to make matters worse back home, my brother Brock went to the hospital with a concussion today. He got hit by a light fixture during a set change." Scarlett remembered the strange text from him this afternoon, asking her to pick him up at the hospital.

Almost like he'd forgotten she was in Los Angeles.

With his arm draped along the back of the love seat, Logan toyed with a lock of her hair, winding it around his finger where it lay on her shoulder.

His touch was one beautiful thing in a day from

hell, and she let the joy of that touch surround her. Heat her skin.

"Your family is struggling with a lot right now," he told her gently. "Are you sure you don't want me to take you to Cheyenne? We could get a private flight and leave tonight."

She appreciated that he was looking out for her. That he cared. Her breath caught for a moment as she glanced toward him. He was incredibly good looking. And those green eyes were only for her.

Her heartbeat quickened.

"I've got a better idea." She wanted to kiss him. Was that wrong of her on a day when everything was falling apart? Maybe that's what love was supposed to be, though.

Something good you could count on even when everything else went wrong.

"You do?" He wound the curl tighter around his finger, tugging gently.

"My mother is still recovering from a coma and clearly doesn't want to talk about her past. But her father—Emilio Ventura—is right here in town." Scarlett was the only one of her mother's daughters who lived close enough to confront the man. "I'll go see him."

"Scarlett." Logan relinquished the lock of hair, already shaking his head. "The Ventura compound will be crawling with paparazzi."

"I'll go incognito." She wanted to be an actress, after all. She'd act her way in there.

"If he's anything like his son, I'm not sure you want to go alone." Logan's voice had a warning note, but she'd just broken away from her overprotective brothers.

She was making her own decisions now.

"I'll find out for myself if my mother is really the missing Hollywood heiress, Eden Harris." Even as she said it, she knew it had to be true. The photos didn't lie. "More importantly, I'll find out why she felt the need to run away from her family and go into hiding for over twenty years." It was the first time all day she'd felt like she had a sense of purpose. A role to play in the family drama exploding all over the news. "If something—or someone—hurt her, I will find out."

An hour into the family meeting, Brock knew he'd made a mistake joining the rest of the McNeills at his father's house. He sat in the recliner closest to the door and wondered when he could make his exit. He didn't want to abandon his dad, stepmother or his siblings, but the ache in his head had shifted from physical pain to a gnawing fear that this injury wasn't like others he'd experienced.

Closing his eyes, he tried to shut out the discussion with the New York–based public relations consultant flown in the day before at Brock's grandfather's request. That was Brock's first indication that something was seriously amiss. It was one thing to forget the seductive actress, Hannah, since by her admission they'd only just met. But to have forgotten that his stubborn father had mended his estrangement with Brock's grandfather, Malcolm McNeill, after a rift that had spanned most of Brock's life?

He couldn't begin to remember how that had occurred. Yet all his siblings behaved like having Malcolm—and Malcolm's girlfriend, Rose—under the same roof as Donovan was no big deal. The extended family filled the living area to capacity, with Maisie and Madeline seated at the kitchen bar so they could be a part of the conversation.

Brock pinched the bridge of his nose, willing his thoughts to realign, his brain to make some kind of order out of the chaos of information floating around him. Strangely, despite the family drama and the very real news that his father's twenty-six-year marriage couldn't be legally recognized anymore if Paige was really Eden Harris, Brock's thoughts returned most often to Hannah.

Was that because being with Hannah was less frustrating since they had very little history together, and therefore, less for him to forget? Or did he think of her more because she made a strong impact on him? She had been beside him when no one else could be today. She'd driven him home. Wished him well.

Maybe that had been all that happened between them on the surface. But he'd felt a whole other layer of things sparking when she'd touched him. She'd meant it to be consoling. Compassionate.

Yet her hand on his arm had stirred a far more elemental response. And he couldn't shake the idea that her gray eyes hid secrets he needed to unlock.

"Donovan, they *need* to know." A soft, feminine voice from the edge of the living room suddenly distinguished itself in the rumble of conversation, quieting the McNeill family instantly.

Brock's stepmother stood framed in the hallway arch, dressed in a blue floral nightgown with a matching cotton robe, her feet bare and her long brown hair unbound. His father had his arm slung around her. She looked pale and physically frail after the weeks in bed recovering from her fall and a coma—events Brock had only learned about today. But there was a glint in her brown eyes.

A fierce light Brock hadn't seen before.

Madeline moved closer to them.

"Can we get you something, Mom?" She gestured toward the kitchen. "A drink? Some tea, maybe?"

Brock leaned forward in the recliner to hear whatever Paige had to say. Was the news true? His stepmother had always been mild-mannered, almost to a fault, given the way she allowed her strong-willed husband's opinions to rule the household. It seemed hard to believe she had masterminded a scheme to assume a new identity as a teenager, moving halfway across the country and marrying a well-known man in Cheyenne without anyone questioning her past.

Then again, the so-called missing Hollywood

heiress had never been formally reported as missing. She'd simply stopped appearing in public.

"No thank you, sweetheart. I just wanted you to know." She glanced from Brock's father toward everyone else in the room, sweeping the living room with her gaze. "All of you. It's true, what the tabloids are saying about me." Her voice trembled a little, and she stopped, then tried again. "I didn't use a new name with the intent to deceive anyone. I just…needed a fresh start."

When the room remained quiet, the public relations consultant—Jasmine—looked ready to ask a question. She drew in a breath and opened her mouth, but Carson was seated next to her and he clamped a firm hand on the woman's arm, effectively silencing her.

Donovan hugged Paige closer to his side. "As far as I'm concerned, her name doesn't change the kind of wife and mother she's been. And a news story about the past doesn't alter who she is on the inside." He turned from Paige to stare at the rest of them. "I know everyone else feels the same way."

A chorus of agreement and support echoed around the room. Maisie darted around her sister to hug their mother.

Paige's eyes were bright as she nodded. "Thank you."

Donovan gently turned her around, guiding her back down the hallway, away from the living area. "Focus on getting well," he told her softly, his words dissolving before they disappeared into the room at the far end of the corridor.

"I can't believe she kept her past a secret our whole lives." Madeline, the oldest of the daughters Brock's father had with his second wife, shook her head in the hallway, looking lost.

Brock knew someone should offer comfort. Words of wisdom. But tonight, with his head throbbing and his thoughts too damn scattered, he couldn't be that guy. The last thing his family needed was to discover he'd lost his memories for at least—as far as he could tell—the last six months. He could recall delivering two fillies to a neighbor with twin girls just after the New Year, but couldn't come up with a memory after that.

Until he woke up with Hannah Ryder staring down at him with concern and secrets in her eyes.

He was pulled out of his thoughts about Hannah when Jasmine tapped a manicured fingernail on the maple dining table to get everyone's attention. "If we're going to get on top of this, we need to issue a statement from the family as quickly as possible."

"Agreed, my dear," Malcolm announced in a weary-sounding voice from his spot beside his girl-friend on one of the sofas. "But as you can see, it's not easy for us to focus on where to go next when we're still reeling with what this means for all of us."

"We could try a diversion tactic until we've come up with a statement," Jasmine suggested. The woman was apparently a friend of Malcom's grandson, Quinn, and his ballerina wife, Sofia Koslov McNeill. Jasmine had done some PR for the dancer before her marriage to Quinn, helping to boost the woman's profile in the dance world.

That news was, perhaps, fresher in Brock's mind than everyone else's. To him, it felt like the Manhattan branch of the family had been making headlines just last week.

Cody, the older of the twins, rose from his chair at the table and stared out the front window toward the driveway and the darkened fields beyond. "Are you suggesting we manufacture a story to take the spotlight off us?"

"Not manufacture." Jasmine sounded offended. "It has to be a real story, but something big enough to change the narrative. Maybe news about a land deal, or some kind of update about the film?"

Brock wasn't cut out for this kind of thing on a good day. And today had sucked the will—and the memories—right out of him. He needed to get out of the house where all the talk of the blackmail scheme and the film confused him. Figure out how in the hell he was going to combat amnesia.

And coax Hannah Ryder into helping him remember what had happened between them, since that memory promised to be more enticing than any other.

"I can't do this now," he announced to the room at large, regretting that he couldn't be a better family member on a day when his siblings needed him.

"My head is throbbing and I can't think straight, so I'm not going to be any help to the cause tonight."

It wouldn't be the first time he'd been a disappointment to his father. The youngest son who flew under the radar was also the one who contributed the least to the ranching operations. Brock's quarter horse program wasn't about raising cattle or increasing herd production.

But it was what he knew best.

Pivoting on his heel, he headed for the exit, already making plans to text Hannah. He'd take a good horse from his father's stable to ride home, unconcerned about the doctor's orders since he was practically born in a saddle. He'd ride past the cabin where Hannah said she was staying since she was practically on the way.

As he was turning the handle, a knock sounded from the other side of the door. He opened it to find a slender brunette in running shorts and a sweatshirt. Her cheeks were pink, her forehead glistening like she'd been sweating. Her eyes were a little bloodshot, like maybe she'd been crying.

"Hey, Brock," she said softly, edging past him into the room.

He had no idea who she was.

But the way Carson charged toward her, concern etched on his features, told Brock it was someone important to the younger of the twins.

"Emma, what's wrong?"

Brock hesitated to leave when everyone else's eyes

were glued on the newcomer as Carson wrapped her in his arms.

"It's my mother," she said, glancing around the room at the rest of the family, her gaze finally settling on him. "Brock, you weren't here three days ago when I was sitting with your mother and recognized the picture in her locket—it's of the woman we now know is her mother, Barbara Harris."

Brock knew the locket his stepmother had always worn. But how the hell could one of Carson's girlfriends identify the face of an actress who hadn't made a film in decades? He nodded, though, unwilling to give away how lost he was, how thoroughly his memories had been stolen by the blow to his head. Although he had to admit, all of this news would be hard to follow even on a normal day.

"I called Mom to talk to her about it since she worked as a maid in the Venturas' home for years." Emma used her long sleeve to swipe at her eyes. "And it turns out Mom is in town. She flew here—to Cheyenne—the day before the second blackmail note was delivered to Paige."

A silence followed. And when no more explanation seemed forthcoming, Maisie stepped closer to Emma.

"I don't understand." Maisie's uncomprehending gaze went from Emma to Carson and back again. "Your mom missed you? She came to see the filming?"

"It's not that." Sniffling, Emma shook her head

and straightened. "My mother had an affair with her boss—Emilio Ventura—long ago. She's always been a little obsessed with him, and she's fought manic depressive disorder my whole life," she clarified. "The fact that my mother is here, in Cheyenne, when the demand for money was sent to Paige from this town, makes me very concerned that my mother could be the blackmailer."

Six

As he left his father's house, Brock gave up trying to put the pieces of the blackmail drama together. He wouldn't be any help tonight when he couldn't even identify some of the people in the room.

Maisie made a half-hearted effort to call him back to the house, asking if he was okay or if he needed a ride home. But his father's stable would have a horse that could get him home. The animals raised on-site made the trek between the Black Creek Ranch and the Creek Spill with regularity, and Brock's house was in between, right on the river.

Not to mention, he'd trained most of the quarter horses personally for the past six years. His successful breeding and training program had given him his own domain within the ranching operation, allowing him autonomy despite all the ways the McNeill businesses intersected and overlapped.

Even concussed and suffering amnesia, he understood horses far better than his family.

He saddled a buckskin mare, Aurora, in the closest stall, taking pleasure from the details he remembered about the animal's heritage, facts that came to mind easily. She was five years old, and one of the offspring of the ranch's most prolific sire. Smart and athletic, Aurora was everything Brock enjoyed about the breed.

When he led her outside into the cool summer night, he had only to nudge her in the direction of the path to his house—a finished home now, according to the photos he'd seen in his phone. The last Brock recalled, he had been framing in the walls, so to see the thing finished had been jarring. He was anxious to see it in person, to see if those photos were real.

The mare responded with a brisk pace and soft snort. Brock straightened in the saddle, the pain in his head receding for the first time in hours as the scent of meadow grasses and wildflowers drifted on the night breeze. He could hear the babble of the creek as they neared the shallow water, and some of the tightness in his chest eased.

As they reached the turnoff that would lead to the cabin where he knew Hannah must be staying, Brock leaned back in the saddle, slowing Aurora to a walk. He hadn't texted her, so she wouldn't be expecting him.

But he could ride past to see if her lights were on. He owed her a thank-you at the very least. Their parting had been strained after he'd been blindsided by the news of his stepmother's identity. He hadn't been at his best.

Now, veering away from the water, Brock guided Aurora through a dense thicket. Big box elders gave way to elm trees and then a few scrubby pines before the land flattened and grazing meadows appeared in the moonlight. Lamps glowed from within the cabin and a hurricane lantern flickered on the patio table of the narrow porch.

Anticipation fired through him. The remnants of the day's headache dissipated at the thought of seeing Hannah.

"Hello?" she called out through the dark as he discerned the figure seated in one of the Adirondack chairs. "Who's there?"

He could hear the tension in her voice. Worry.

"It's Brock." He regretted surprising her, and lifted a hand in greeting as Aurora neared the cabin. "I didn't mean to startle you. I'm just on my way home."

To see the house he'd built himself, but for the most part couldn't remember building.

Hannah gave a soft laugh as she rose to her feet and stepped down onto the grass. "I'm not used to hearing big animals heading toward me in the dark."

She stopped short of the horse. Hannah wore a pale, hooded sweatshirt that said I Read Past My Bedtime in bright pink letters. She reached up to stroke the animal's nose as Brock swung down to the ground.

With her face scrubbed clean and her hair pulled back in a low ponytail that rested on her shoulder, she looked relaxed. Maybe ready for bed. His brain ran wild, his thoughts unchecked for a moment before he reined himself in. He stood close to her in the tall grass, the clean scent of her hair close enough for him to breathe in.

He forgot what he'd come here to say. His attention was focused solely on her. Being here felt right. Familiar.

Being with her would feel even better.

She glanced up at him suddenly, gray eyes zeroing in on his. "I wasn't expecting to see you again today."

How come the most ordinary interactions with Brock McNeill felt hotter—sexier—than blatant kisses she'd shared with other men?

Hannah tried to get ahold of her wayward libido by reminding herself why she'd lied to Brock about being with him the night before. She could not afford to be in a relationship with a man whose family had a kinship with her enemy.

It wasn't easy to keep that in mind given how different the two men seemed. But she wasn't in Cheyenne to indulge herself. She was only here to save her sister Hope from falling any further into a dark pit of unhappiness.

Brock sidestepped her, taking the horse's reins and dropping them to the ground.

"I realized I didn't thank you for all you did for me." He was still in the same clothes he'd worn earlier that day at the hospital. He had to be exhausted after the time in the emergency room and the scandal breaking with his family.

"You're welcome. It was no trouble since they canceled shooting to work on the lights." She knew the filming in Cheyenne was going to run over budget and over schedule. Which was just as well since it gave her more time to speak privately with members of the cast to find other victims of Antonio Ventura's predatory behavior. "I don't know how you're still functioning after the day you've had."

Brock lifted a hand to touch the back of his head, muscles flexing in a way that stirred something in the pit of her belly.

"I feel better," he admitted. "Actually, getting out of my father's house and away from the drama helped air out some of the cobwebs in my brain."

A sliver of panic froze her.

"Are you—" Her voice cracked. "I mean, is your memory returning?" What would she say if he asked her why she lied to him about what happened the night before?

A McNeill was a powerful enemy to make. A word in the director's ear could get her fired.

He studied her for a long moment before shaking his head. "I'm struggling to remember anything that's happened after January."

Relieved, she all but sagged onto the porch's wooden stair railing. Still, she couldn't deny a pang of empathy for him. She couldn't imagine losing a whole chunk of your life that way.

"I'm sorry." She hugged her arms around herself; the wind off the mountains was surprisingly cold once the sun went down. "And I'm sure your family couldn't be much help tonight with all the news about your stepmom."

"Are you cold?" he asked, his gaze dipping to her body as she shivered. "There's gas in the fire pit, you know." He pointed to the small stone ring with a slate mantel. "Unless you'd be more comfortable indoors."

Ever since she'd practically dragged him over the threshold into the cabin last night, the place was full of memories starring him. So indoors was not a good idea.

"A fire sounds great," she told him. "But the remote for it might be inside. I didn't read any of the instructions on operating things like that."

Brock was up the stairs and beside the fire pit a moment later. "You can switch it on manually." He reached under the slate mantel and must have found the button because there was a whoosh of orange-and-blue flame from the center of the ring.

Hannah followed him onto the porch, which was just big enough for two chairs, a love seat and the fire pit. There was a ground level patio area where she did yoga in the mornings. The views were incredible.

"This is perfect." She held her hands out to the open flame, warming them. "Thank you."

"No problem." He stood on the opposite side of the fire pit, watching her. "And as for my family not being much help with my memories—you're right. Today, the focus was very much on my stepmother."

"How is she doing?" She wanted to know if the rest of his family had been surprised by the news, or if they'd been well aware of her relationship to the Ventura family.

"I'm honestly not sure how much I'm supposed to say outside the family." He stepped around the fire pit to stand closer to her, the heat and strength of him near enough to touch. "My grandfather brought in a public relations consultant to help us figure out our next move."

"That makes sense." She shivered again, but this time it had nothing to do with the chill in the air and everything to do with his proximity. "The McNeill name is highly recognizable. You'll want to protect the brand."

He shrugged, his gaze moving over her. "It's more of a worry for the resort business than the ranching operations, I would think. And for my part, I can't imagine why anyone looking for a good horse would suddenly decide they shouldn't buy from me because my stepmother is a runaway Hollywood heiress."

"People want to know they're dealing with someone honest. Forthright." She wondered if he really believed his business would be unaffected or if he was trying to look at the bright side. There was no doubt in her mind the scandal would have an impact. "And an association with the Venturas is a dubious distinction. The family might carry industry clout, but they aren't well liked."

"You're right, of course." His lips curved in a humorless smile. "There's bound to be a business impact. I had hoped my head had cleared with some fresh air, but I'm still not thinking straight." He turned more fully toward her. "Can I ask one more favor of you, Hannah?"

Hearing him speak her name tripped pleasantly over her nerve endings. Her throat dried up.

"Sure." She peered up at him, keeping her body facing the fire and not him.

"Maybe it's because we haven't known each other long and we don't have a history. But I find it easier to talk to you than anyone in my family right now."

"You do?" His words shot arrows of guilt into her since they absolutely had a history. She tucked her hands into the pocket of her hoodie, afraid he'd see them shaking.

"Definitely." His blue eyes simmered with the same fire that had scorched her the night before. "It's less pressure to talk to you, and you don't make my head hurt."

"Oh." She knew what was coming and wanted to cut him off, since the less time she spent with him, the better. But how could she tell him that? How could she say that being with him was a constant battle not to touch him? Kiss him? Think about the times he'd touched and kissed her?

"Have dinner with me this week. When you're off, or else after you're done working for the day."

"I. Um—" She tried to think of a compelling reason why she couldn't. But as he reached to graze a touch along her cheek, it was all she could do not to close her eyes and sway into him.

His eyes turned serious. "I know I wouldn't have confided in you about someone blackmailing my family if I didn't trust you. If I didn't want…something more with you."

She straightened, needing to do damage control. Fast.

"I didn't get that impression at all," she protested. "You were just being kind to bring me home last night."

"Hannah." His voice was softly chiding, his knuckle lingering on her cheek in the barest of touches. "Even now, I feel more than that between us. Having amnesia doesn't keep me from knowing I would have been every bit as attracted to you yesterday, too."

How could she argue with that logic? Denying it felt like swimming against a riptide. She didn't have a chance.

"Attracted or not, I'm not sure it's wise." She

wanted to follow that up with a compelling argument. She had none she could share with him.

"Don't say yes to dinner with me because it's *wise*. Say yes because you want to get to know me." He leaned closer, his gaze falling to her mouth. "Or because you don't want to go your whole life without kissing a cowboy." For a moment, they breathed the same air. Her eyelids fluttered. "Or hell, say yes because we both need to eat, and I can promise you better food than you'll get from the film's dining services."

He let his hand fall away from her, giving her space to decide.

And how could she refuse? He was right about the attraction, of course. But the main reason she wanted to see him again was to keep an eye on the situation. To know if he recovered his memories. To find out why his stepmother had run from the Ventura household at a young age.

It wasn't about kissing a cowboy, damn it.

Because she already knew exactly how good that felt.

"You make a convincing argument," she told him finally. "I'm done filming most days by seven."

Hannah was still thinking about that impending date late the next morning as she walked the short distance from her cabin to the day's filming location.

She wore a simple sundress and a hat wide enough to keep the freckles at bay in the intense Wyoming sun. Brock had told her he'd message her today once he'd made reservations for dinner. Considering his thoughtfulness, it was too bad her relationship with him was destined for an unhappy end. Most of the guys Hannah had dated in the past were content to go out with a pack of friends rather than make special plans for a one-on-one evening out.

So the fact that Brock wanted to do something nice for her slid right under her defenses. That, coupled with the way he'd put Antonio in his place that first day they'd met, set him apart from most men. In particular, men of wealth and privilege. In her experience, men born with that kind of advantage in life rarely saw past their own comfort.

Witness her father, a prestigious attorney who'd gladly cut off his daughters from the family fortune when he'd walked out on their mother. Not that Hannah cared for herself. But for Hope's sake? It still made her furious a decade after he'd left. Her father had made mincemeat of his ex-wife's divorce lawyer, his precious money well protected from the family he no longer wanted.

Hannah's phone chimed, and she dug in her bag for it, glad for the distraction from the dark thoughts. She glanced at the caller ID, feeling a charge of anticipation as she wondered if it would be Brock. Her sister's number flashed on the screen instead. Instantly worried, she hurried to answer.

"Hi, Hope." She injected a brightness into her

voice she didn't feel before carefully asking, "How are you doing?"

Her sister had moved in with her when she'd turned eighteen, after graduating high school, when their mother announced her plan to go "live her own life" and travel. But Hannah had loved having Hope around. She'd bought them matching rings and told Hope it was them against the world—the Ryder team. Hope attended community college for two years before switching to taking classes at UCLA—classes she'd once been so excited about. Lately, Hannah had to remind her to get out the door to attend them.

"Honestly? I'm not great, Hannah." Hope sounded wound up. More upset than usual. The last few months she'd retreated into days of near-silence, so hearing her voice so animated now put Hannah on alert. "*Winning the West* is all over the news. His face—it's everywhere."

Hannah's brain raced to fill in the blanks. She stopped in the middle of the grassy trail that led to the day's shooting location—a rocky gully where a secret meeting was taking place among three of the film's characters. She still had time before she needed to be in the makeup chair.

"Why? Because of the Eden Harris story?" She guessed it had something to do with the scandal. "I mean, has there been any more news today?"

"I don't know!" Hope spoke in a loud whisper, as if she was trying to be quiet and failing. In the background, shrill pop music blared. She must be at the mall where she had a job in a teen clothing shop. "But all the girls at work keep showing me videos of the ranch where you're shooting because they know you're in the film. And his stupid face is always there."

A new fear crawled up her spine. Tension pulled at her shoulders. Did Brock know about this?

"There's footage of the ranch?" Hannah charged in the direction of the shoot, worried what she might find. "As in, the tabloids are up here now?"

She hadn't checked her media feeds this morning. She'd been too busy enjoying the Zen-like atmosphere of waking up in a country cabin, sipping her coffee in the quiet as she watched the sun come up over the field.

"They keep showing clips of...*him* outside a cowboy bar. Someone asks him if he knew Mrs. McNeill was really Eden Harris when he decided to film in Cheyenne." Hope lowered her voice more as she rushed on, "I don't know why you had to do this, Hannah. I never wanted you to have anything to do with him."

Hannah hated that she was hurting her sister more. But she had to believe she was doing the right thing in the long run.

"Honey, I would have been an extra in this movie to work with him. You know that." She strained to see the film set in the distance, wondering if she should be looking for drone cameras or photographers in the bushes. "I'm going to find evidence of the kind of person he is. Once he's publicly exposed as a predator, he won't be able to hurt anyone else again."

She thought about texting the wardrobe assistant, Callie, to see if there was any news about paparazzi near the ranch, but it was hard to see her screen in direct sun. And if she messaged anyone, maybe it should be Brock. His family would want to know about this if they weren't already aware.

Then again, Brock said they'd hired a public relations manager. So they must know. For that matter, maybe the McNeills were leveraging the notoriety for business reasons. The thought of Brock having a connection to Antonio Ventura—of possibly profiting from it—made her ill.

"And in the meantime, the man who hurt me is your boss. Whenever I think about you working for him—"

Hannah couldn't hear the rest.

Because as the filming location came into view, so did a crowd outside the wardrobe tent. A ring of people standing and watching something in their midst. Something Hannah couldn't see.

"Hope, I promise I'll be careful." She picked up her pace, jogging through the grass as the trail flattened out. "But I really need to go. I'm due on set right now, okay?"

Disconnecting the call, she raced toward the throng of people—production assistants, wardrobe and makeup staffers, writers, transportation crew, animal handlers. Everyone seemed to be gathered around something. A fight? A member of the media?

But as she skidded to a halt behind the pack, Hannah could hear a man speaking. It was Antonio Ventura.

"—and if that's what it takes to get everyone on this production on the same page, I will do it," he was saying, his voice taking on a vaguely threatening tone. "I've done it on other film sets."

A murmur went through the group and Hannah wondered exactly what he was proposing to get them "on the same page." She sidled closer to Callie and tried to get a better view of the man she despised.

Callie, seeing her, covered one side of her mouth to whisper, "Says he's holding our cell phones hostage if we're not good girls and boys."

The director took his time glaring around at every member of the assembled group. "The added media attention is only a problem if we make it one. I will view anyone who posts updates from this set, or who publicly speculates about the Ventura family, as someone who has no interest in working with me— or this production company—again."

He stormed off toward a production trailer, one of his assistants scrambling to catch up.

He's reaching, Hannah wanted to shout to the younger crewmembers, to let the newbies know that a director didn't have that kind of hold over a production company. Ventura couldn't dictate whom that company hired for future projects. But, selfishly,

Hannah appreciated that the unrest on set might result in her overhearing something damning about Antonio sooner rather than later. An unhappy cast and crew would create a better environment for one of Ventura's victims to let her guard down about the man's behavior.

So Hannah said nothing, listening as the crowd broke up. Some people seemed to think it was all grandstanding to get cooperation, but Hannah also heard someone start to recount the reports from one of Antonio's overseas productions where he did indeed collect the cast's phones, holding on to them for weeks.

As the group thinned out and people began returning to their work, Callie walked with Hannah to the makeup trailer, then held the door for her as they stepped inside the mobile unit.

"So what prompted the tirade?" Hannah asked as she dropped into the makeup chair, settling her bag under the mirrored table in front of her.

They were the only ones in the vintage Airstream. The hair and makeup people must have been lingering to talk after the director's mini-meltdown. Hannah wanted to open her media feeds and catch up on the news from the set since Hope had mentioned a lot of media focus on the film. But sometimes scrolling through a feed sent the message that you didn't want to talk, and Hannah couldn't afford to have people shut her out. She needed confidences if she was ever going to collect damning evidence against Antonio.

"One of the extras posted a photo of Antonio side by side with a photo of Paige McNeill, both of them standing in front of the Creek Spill Ranch welcome sign," Callie explained, reaching to straighten the collar on the shirt that Hannah would be wearing in the day's scene. "The extra added a caption that said, 'Separated at birth?' because they were both wearing jeans and a Stetson."

"Doesn't sound like a big deal to me."

"It shouldn't have been, except that Antonio looks like a sloppy, lewd old man in his photo, with his T-shirt barely covering his gut, while Eden Harris is still as lovely as ever. Since the two of them are close in age, it's my guess Antonio's ego took a hit."

Lewd? The word caught Hannah's attention more than anything else the wardrobe assistant said. Had Callie seen inappropriate behavior from the director? She promised herself that she would circle back to the subject.

"I thought he was angry because there are tabloid reporters in Cheyenne." She debated grabbing her phone now to see what else she could unearth online. Also, she wondered if Brock had messaged her, because he was never far from her thoughts today. "My sister said there's a lot of talk about the filming since the news broke yesterday about Eden Harris."

Callie nodded, dropping onto a bench seat across from Hannah, her long ponytail draping down her arm. "Everyone in Hollywood wants to find out if the Ventura family knew where Eden was all this time since no one ever formally reported her missing. She just sort of disappeared."

Hannah's phone vibrated. She could hear the soft buzz even with the device in her bag. But her attention went to the door of the trailer as one of the production assistants stuck his head in.

"Filming is canceled today, ladies. Security breach at the front gate of the ranch. The McNeill family has recommended we wait a day to film until they get the ranch borders secured."

A second later, the man was gone, no doubt off to spread the news.

Callie clapped her hands together. "Free day!" she shouted, doing a dance on the trailer floor before hopping out the door, too fast for Hannah to stop her or ask about the "lewd" comment. Darn it.

She reached for her bag instead, pulling out the phone to see that a text message had arrived from her date tomorrow.

Security issues mean we can't readily go to a five-star location. I'm importing a five-star chef to my home instead. I'll pick you up tomorrow night at seven thirty.

Hannah read the message twice, her heart pounding. Dinner at Brock's home sounded intimate. Decadent.

She'd have to be very, very careful that she used the time to learn more about him, and not fall further under his seductive spell.

Seven

Brock hadn't wanted to pick up his date with a security detail trailing him. But considering the swarm of paparazzi looking for a way onto McNeill lands since yesterday, he'd finally agreed to have one of the extra guards follow him over to Hannah's cabin. Brock had enough on his mind tonight without running interference with the media if reporters managed to infiltrate the Creek Spill Ranch.

And to the guard's credit, Brock didn't even see anyone else around when he halted in front of the cabin in his pickup truck. Switching off the headlights and the engine, he left the keys on the seat before striding toward the cabin.

Music drifted from the windows, a sweetly haunting aria sung in a foreign language, and not at all what he would have expected from Hannah's playlist. Not that he knew much about her outside the compelling draw between them. Still, he looked forward to learning more about this woman who felt strangely like a calm center in the storm of amnesia, blackmail and scandal.

He'd spent most of the previous day with his neurologist, discussing the results of the CT scan and trying to get answers about his memories. The consultation hadn't given him anything more concrete than he'd learned in the ER, but at least his headache had eased. He'd met with his family again the night before, and the publicist had announced a new family story for redirecting public interest. Malcolm McNeill had proposed to his girlfriend, Rose Hanson, and the pair had revealed a Manhattan wedding planned for the end of the month.

Brock might not remember anything about his grandfather before the last two days, but he had to admit the patriarch of the McNeill clan knew how to put family first. The announcement of the billionaire's late-in-life remarriage had eased some of the intense interest in Paige's Hollywood past.

Now, before Brock could knock on Hannah's door, it opened with a sudden flood of lamplight and a faint hint of orange blossoms. His date appeared on the threshold.

A silky dress swirled around her, strapless and floor length in color blocks of bright purple, fuchsia and pink. A gold lamé belt wrapped the slimmest part of her, while gold shoes peeked out from the pink hem. Her long blond waves were curled in neat coils.

"Brock." Her smile seemed genuine, her tone relieved. "After filming was canceled, I've been worried there would be a rush of photographers if I so much as cracked the door open." Her gaze skittered past him to peer out into the dark. "But there's no one out there?"

"There's a security detail at the tree line." He couldn't peel his attention away from her. "You look beautiful."

"Thank you." Her hands fluttered nervously as she hurried to pick up a remote from the coffee table. Stabbing at it, she silenced the swelling violins of the opera music. "I packed only so much for the trip, but luckily, I had a dress."

She retrieved a small gold clutch and slid her keycard inside before she switched off the wrought iron chandelier in the living area. Brock scanned the room to make sure the place looked secure before they left. Now that the ranch had become a point of interest for the tabloids, he regretted that she was staying in the cabin alone. Vulnerable.

His gaze snagged on the door to the bedroom toward the back. He had a sudden vision of them there, kissing at the threshold of that door, before falling into the bed that awaited—

"… Brock?" Hannah asked, staring at him intently. She worried her lower lip, nibbling one side for a moment before speaking again. "Is everything okay?"

How long had he been standing there, fantasizing about a moment that felt all too real? He shook off the sensation of being caught in a memory that wouldn't come. No doubt he had daydreamed about that scenario when he accompanied Hannah to this cabin before, the way she'd described. His desire for her was sharp, but that didn't mean he would act on it too fast. He looked forward to spending time with her first. Getting to know her.

"Better than okay." He had gone to considerable effort to arrange this evening with her. He refused to make a mess of it before they even set foot in his house. "I've been looking forward to this all day."

Offering her his arm, he guided her out of the cabin and into the summer night. The breeze stirred the silky layers of her dress, blowing it against him as he helped her into the truck, stirring awareness all over again.

Resolutely, he trained his focus on the grassy road that led to his place, needing to stay alert. He saw no one on the way, not even the security guard. His home was more remote than either of his brothers' since he'd chosen a tract of land near the Black Creek between the two main ranches, so perhaps that accounted for the quiet. But his brother Carson had also assured him the security team was top-notch when they messaged earlier in the day. Apparently, Carson had invested in a private security firm before he'd allowed the production company to film up here in the first place. Then, after Carson's girlfriend's shocking announcement the night before about her mother potentially being the blackmailer, Carson had hired even more guards to make sure Emma's mother, Jane Layton, didn't come near McNeill property.

When Brock cleared the final bend before his house, Hannah gasped.

"What's wrong?" He turned to look at her, but she was staring out the front windshield.

"That's your house?" She glanced toward him and raised her eyebrows. "Brock, it's gorgeous."

He wasn't sure that he'd describe it quite that way, but still, her words were flattering. "Thank you. I worked on this place for years, and I'm finding it frustrating that now I can't recall finishing the building."

Parking the truck close to the front entrance so she wouldn't have far to walk, he got out, pocketed the keys and went around to help her from the vehicle.

"You built this?" she asked as she stepped carefully down from the running board onto the flagstones beneath.

He held one of her hands, feeling the softness of her creamy skin, curbing the impulse to stroke his thumb over her palm. Letting her go, he shut the door behind her and stood beside her to stare up at the house.

At almost eight thousand square feet, there was

plenty of room. Much of the first level had a river stone facade, the gray rocks blending with the retaining walls and footpaths that led up from the Black Creek. The porch posts on the first level were stone, but the wide porches of the second level were wooden, the two materials blending in a proportion that felt right for a house set against the woods and overlooking a wide creek. Now, with all of the outdoor and landscaping lights on, the house was reflected in the calm water.

"I did most of it. I contracted out the plumbing and electrical. And I had a professional excavator help me with the site's foundation. But the rest was all me." He had, at least, painstakingly preserved the effort in photos. If he never recovered the missing gap in his memories, he had the photo history. "For years, this was my second job after I finished working with the horses."

The scents of smoked pancetta and roasted hen drifted from the kitchen, a reminder that appetizers would be served shortly. Brock led her into the house, explaining a few of the features she asked about on the way, like the beams in the cathedral ceiling of the foyer and the hand-cut logs used as supports in the main archway that led to the kitchen.

They avoided the kitchen, however, since he'd given over the gourmet facility to the chef and her staff for the night. Brock had asked for the meal to be served upstairs on the covered balcony overlooking the Black Creek, a vaulted veranda with an outdoor fireplace already lit to ensure they were comfortable even in the night chill.

"This is incredible." Hannah spun in a slow circle to take in the balcony with its round dining table already set for two. Three white candles burned under a hurricane globe surrounded by sunflowers, roses and orange lilies.

Brock was satisfied that his preparations were to her liking. He only wished he'd hired musicians for the night since he would have liked the opportunity to dance with her. It would have given him a reason to wrap her in his arms.

"I'm sorry we couldn't go out tonight." He hadn't ever met a woman he wanted to romance to this degree. Not that he remembered, anyhow.

His phone hadn't revealed any liaisons in the past six months. He would guess he'd poured all his free time into finishing the house.

Hannah set her gold clutch on an end table by the fireplace. "Who wants to go out when you have this sort of luxury at home?"

"Maybe." Brock strode over to the champagne bucket on a silver stand beside the dining table. "Can I pour you champagne?" He turned the label of the bottle toward him. "The wines are the only elements of the meal I chose tonight. The chef picked everything else."

"In that case, yes." Hannah strode closer, her pink-and-purple gown fluttering around her and brushing against him. "Just a little, though, since I have to work tomorrow."

"I wouldn't be so sure." Brock used a towel to hold the cork as he opened the bottle. "Your director threatened to pack up the whole shoot and return to LA to film on a studio lot if we can't do more to ensure privacy here."

He poured the champagne into two glasses as a waiter entered with a tray of appetizers and discreetly left it on the table. Brock had ordered a tasting menu that would ensure new dishes were brought often, in small portions, since he hadn't been certain of her preferences.

"You've spoken with Antonio?" Hannah asked, her soft fingers grazing his as she accepted a crystal champagne flute. Was that worry he detected in her voice? Perhaps she was concerned about her job, or the quality of the film if the director abandoned the location.

"No, I haven't." Settling the bottle back into the ice, he picked up his glass and led her toward the screened stone hearth where a fire crackled and popped. "Antonio sent a message to my brother Carson, which he shared with the family. The director of *Winning the West* hasn't made a good impression with the McNeills, and we will be glad when he leaves." Brock leaned closer to Hannah, tipping his forehead near hers. "The same can't be said of you."

She glanced up, firelight playing over her delicate features as she gazed into his eyes. He wanted to pluck her glass from her fingers and kiss her. Taste her lips instead of champagne. He gave himself a moment to contemplate that kiss before he continued.

"I'm in no hurry for you to leave, Hannah," he told her, burning to touch her. Instead, he clinked his glass to hers. "Cheers to us, and whatever time we have together."

Two hours later, seated across the table from Brock McNeill in the loveliest outdoor living space she could have imagined, Hannah thought that if she met him now, she would have never mistaken him for a cowboy.

And not just because of the custom-tailored tuxedo that fit him as comfortably as the denim he'd worn the first time she'd seen him. Though she would have to be blind not to notice the way the rich black fabric of the jacket made his eyes even bluer. There was also something about his whole manner tonight that seemed different.

When he'd given her a ride home on his horse that first night, she'd been the aggressor, falling into his arms and kissing him after the ride because the heat had been so intense, and the stress of the shoot had shredded her defenses. Tonight, she couldn't afford to give in to temptation, so she waited. Watched. This time, Brock made the seductive overtures, and he was far more patient. Thoughtful. While she'd simply thrown herself in his arms, Brock tempted her senses with fine foods and wines, tantalized her intellect with insightful discussion about everything from acting to horses, opera to ranches.

He'd been considerate of her comfort and responsive to her smallest request, taking her on an impromptu tour of the grounds between dinner and dessert when she'd asked about the flowering trees she could see thanks to the landscape lighting. Now, pushing aside the final plate of the evening—a personal fruit sampler with one perfect berry of every kind imaginable—Hannah reminded herself she wasn't here to fall for Brock McNeill.

She had accepted his dinner invitation to learn more about his family's connection to the Venturas, and she couldn't leave until she gleaned something that could help her sister.

"So your grandfather is getting married?" she asked, leaning back in her chair while Brock poured them both more sparkling water from the bottle their waiter had left on the table.

"He is." Brock gestured toward the hearth where a blaze still burned bright. "Would you like to sit by the fire?"

"Sure." She brought her water glass with her, setting it on the wrought iron table in front of the love seat. She made herself comfortable in the deep navy cushions, sitting sideways to converse with him better. Or maybe to face him head-on so his allure didn't catch her by surprise. Slipping off her shoes, she tucked her feet under her. "Malcolm's timing must have been a welcome relief for your family. It seems like talk of a McNeill wedding has shifted a little of the tabloid attention away from your stepmother."

"My grandfather did the family a real kindness," Brock agreed, staring into the flames as he took the seat beside her, his broad shoulder almost close enough that she could have tipped her chin forward to lean on him. "His proposal came at an opportune time. But after seeing him with Rose, I believe he would have married her either way."

"You could tell just by looking at them?" she teased.

He took the question seriously, mulling it over for a minute before he nodded. "There was something in the way they looked at each other. Like they would gravitate toward each other even in a crowded room."

"Oh." The idea stole her breath. Especially coming from this man, who drew her toward him in spite of her best efforts. "That's very romantic."

Suddenly too warm, she leaned forward to retrieve her water, craving a cool drink. Brock's gaze followed her. She could feel it, even if she didn't look his way, focusing instead on the fire.

"I suppose it is," he agreed. "I haven't seen many couples look at each other that way."

"Not even your father and stepmother? They've been together a long time. Or your brothers? I've heard rumors that both Carson and Cody have found the women of their dreams recently."

"You probably know more about my family than I do since I don't remember the last six months." He tipped his head back against the headrest, frustration lacing his voice. "Carson's girlfriend showed up at my father's house the other night and I would have sworn I'd never seen her before."

"I can't imagine how maddening that feels," Hannah admitted, returning her drink to the table. "The only reason I know about your brothers is because of gossip on the set. The McNeill men have been an ongoing source of feminine interest and speculation since I arrived in Cheyenne."

"No one was more surprised than me to learn the twins have settled down." He shifted on the love seat to face her, his knee grazing hers. "And as for my father and stepmother, I always viewed their marriage as one of convenience until I saw them together the other night. My father seemed almost…tender with her. Maybe because of her accident and the coma that she's still recovering from, or maybe he feels bad for her about the scandal."

The warmth of his leg heated her skin right through her dress, the memory of where they'd touched enough to elicit tingly sensations up her thigh. She finally had the conversation directed in a way that might yield useful information about Antonio Ventura, but all she could think about was the awareness pooling inside her. The magnetic draw every time their eyes met.

She had to do better than this. She needed to put Hope first.

"Do you think your father knows why Paige

turned her back on her birth family? Or why she left home in the first place? Over twenty years is a long time to stay away."

Hannah had asked herself those questions many times since the scandal broke. Did the McNeill family hide the connection on purpose? Had they even known about it?

Brock shook his head. "I couldn't say. Paige told us she never meant to deceive us. That she just needed a fresh start. And my father supported her, saying her name didn't change who she is on the inside, which I respect."

Hannah searched his eyes, hungry to know more. Perhaps he simply didn't know. Or maybe the amnesia had compromised his ability to remember the details of the scandal in the days leading up to the breaking news. But no matter how the incident had unfolded, she believed him now. She trusted that Brock hadn't known his stepmother was a relation to Antonio Ventura. Trusted that he wasn't helping Ventura hide behind his famous name and Hollywood power.

Brock's sole concern was for his family. And it hurt to think she'd lost out on a chance to have something more with him—to follow this heat where it led for a second time—when he was an honorable man. A simple rancher who also just happened to be a member of one of the wealthiest families in the country.

"Your father sounds like a good man." With an

effort, she blinked away the haze of attraction, needing to leave before she did something foolish, like kiss him again. "You're lucky to have grown up with that kind of role model."

"You're not close with your father?"

"Not at all." She shook her head, sitting forward on the love seat and sliding her feet back into her shoes. "He walked out on my mother when we were young. He's always been more interested in his career than his family."

"You said 'we.'" Brock fingered a purple silk ruffle where it rested on the love seat, smoothing his thumb along the fabric. "Do you have siblings?"

"Just one sister. Hope." She regretted that the filming, and her absence from LA, was hurting her sister so much. But she couldn't just pack up and go home when someone on this set might know Antonio's secrets. "She's lived with me in LA for the past two years. I'd do anything in the world for her."

Brock's smile was quick and genuine. Understanding. "I'd slay dragons for my sisters, too. So it kills me to think how much this scandal is turning their world upside down." He shook his head, a sadness making his eyes turn a shade bluer. "The legal battles they'll have to fight to maintain their portion of the family lands and inheritance."

The knowledge of how much they shared in common, despite the surface differences, helped Hannah to better understand why she'd been so drawn to him that first night. She might not have known all those layers of his character, but she had sensed a connection immediately. What would have happened if she'd trusted that instinct? If she hadn't lied to him after he'd awoken with amnesia, and instead admitted that they had started a relationship?

Would things be any different now?

"I'm sorry they will have to fight those battles." She reached for him, unable to stop herself from laying her hand on his knee. "I know how much it hurts when you can't fix things for the people you love most."

She'd only meant to empathize. But as she stared into his eyes in the firelight, she felt the current between them strengthen. Deepen.

Flare hotter.

Tugging her hand away, she straightened before things got even more complicated between them.

"I should go," she announced, not surprised that her voice was a throaty rasp. She'd used all her restraint to prevent herself from touching him more. She didn't have anything left to hide the hunger in her tone. "That is, I have an early call tomorrow."

"Of course." Standing, he extended his hand to her and deftly helped her to her feet. "It's been a pleasure having dinner with you."

Was it her imagination, or did he linger over that word *pleasure* a fraction longer than the others? Memories tumbled through her. Touches. Tastes. Whispers.

She remembered all of it so thoroughly she couldn't imagine how he'd forgotten.

Her throat was so dry she couldn't answer. Settling for a nod, she knew she needed to get outside, away from the romantic firelight and the allure of Brock's undivided attention.

Ten minutes later, as the truck pulled up to her cabin, she all but sprinted out, not waiting for him to help her down.

"Thank you for everything," she called over her shoulder, her whole body still on fire from that briefest of touches back at his place. The night air hadn't done anything to cool things down. "Dinner was lovely. I had a nice time."

Brock was beside her a moment later, his long legs and loafers covering ground faster than she could in her open-toe stilettos.

"If the evening was so lovely and nice, Hannah Ryder, I'm not sure why you're racing away like the hounds of hell are at your heels."

He opened the screen door for her, pinning it with his body while she fumbled for her keycard.

"I'm not sprinting." Although if she'd had her running shoes on, she would have definitely moved faster. "I'm just…not in a good position to take things any further."

"And have I done anything to give you the impression I'm the kind of man who would press the issue?" Even in the dark, his eyes flashed with a hint of anger. Hurt.

She'd offended him without intending to.

"Absolutely not." She backed up a step, leaning on one side of the doorjamb while he bracketed the other side with his broad shoulders and brooding looks. She'd tried hiding her feelings and clearly that hadn't worked out well. There was nothing left but to be honest. "My speed has to do with me trying to outrun my own desires, Brock. Not you."

Some of the tension slid from him. "And if you've already explained that to me, keep in mind, I can't remember. Just like everything else that happened between us that first night—my memory of it is gone."

The scents of meadow grasses and wildflowers wafted across the fields, the breeze catching the silk of her dress. She didn't know what to say, but she couldn't talk about that night anymore. Her conscience wouldn't let her misrepresent the truth more than she already had.

"We didn't discuss it that night." She squeezed the metallic gold clutch harder to keep herself from touching him. "But I'm very involved in my sister's life right now, helping her deal with the fallout of a… traumatic experience. This probably wasn't a good time for me to take a movie role, but I'm committed to getting home as soon as I can."

"My sister is in LA, too." He frowned slightly, looking thoughtful. "Scarlett is frustrated with the family for not protecting her mother more, and I worry about her making major life decisions about her future when she's angry."

Hannah was grateful he understood. That he didn't dig deeper into her reasons for not indulging the attraction between them.

"That gives me an idea," Brock said suddenly, straightening from where he'd been leaning against the doorframe opposite her and stepping closer. "If you end up with more days off in the shooting schedule, let me know. We could fly to the West Coast for the day. Check on our siblings." His eyes glittered with unspoken possibilities. "Share another dinner."

The thought of spending more time with him tantalized her even as she knew he needed to be off-limits that way. Licking her lips, she readied an automatic "no." But then, feeling herself sway on knees weak with want, she wondered how foolish she was being to deny herself the pleasure of his touch when he could wake up tomorrow and remember everything that happened that first night anyhow.

One day Brock McNeill would resent her for lying to him. Deservedly so. It wasn't like he would think any more kindly of her if she refused every kiss until then.

Or was she rationalizing wildly for the chance to be with him again?

"Maybe," she said finally, the word scarcely a whisper between them since they were standing far closer than she'd realized.

Drawn together. *Gravitating* toward each other.

He didn't touch her. And wouldn't, she knew,

after how she'd pulled away from him earlier. If she wanted more, she would have to make the next move.

One kiss wouldn't hurt.

She wondered if she'd spoken the thought aloud because his eyes darkened with desire, his gaze moving to her lips. Staying there.

Her heart pounded harder. Faster. Propelling her to take just one taste...

Fingers landing on the bristle of his jaw, she traced the hard edge toward his chin. Swaying closer, she skimmed her hand down the warmth of his neck, curving around the back to where his hair curled against his collar.

And then, she was kissing him. Gently. Sweetly. She nipped and tasted, remembering the feel of his mouth even as the kiss was completely different from that first, no-holds-barred night together. He let her feel and explore, get wrapped up in the taste and textures of their lips brushing. Only when she sighed with pleasure did he give her more. His hand splayed on the base of her spine, a welcome, seductive weight that anchored her against him. Sensations bombarded her, from the warm strength of his chest under his jacket, to the taut muscle of his thigh where it pressed lightly against the inside of her hip.

She clutched at his lapels, straining closer, losing herself in the kiss. His tongue stroked over hers in a way that made her shudder with need. In a way that reminded her how quickly he could take her to the brink, and push her over...

He pulled away then. Slowly. It took her a moment to even register what had happened. Her gaze was fuzzy and unfocused. Her fingers still clenched the silk of his tuxedo as if he was the answer to everything she wanted. Needed. As her senses returned to her, she spied the regret in his eyes that echoed the sentiment tightening in her chest.

With an effort, she disentangled herself from the fabric, easing away from the scent of his aftershave and the taste of his lips. Her skin tingled, and her body hummed with thwarted anticipation.

"I would never press the issue," he reminded her, his fingers lightly combing through her hair before he stepped back, breaking the spell. "But the offer to go to LA is open." He lifted her hand to his mouth and kissed the palm before closing her fingers over the tender place he'd just touched. "Think about it, Hannah."

He settled her forgotten keycard in the door lock and opened it for her before he turned and strode down the steps and back to his truck. Hannah could almost swear she'd forgotten how to breathe until then. Finally, dragging in a gulp of night air, she forced herself to step inside the cabin. Closing the door behind her, she leaned against the barrier for a long moment, knowing she wasn't going to be able to get that kiss out of her mind.

Brock had told her to think about a trip to LA.

Tonight, she'd be lucky if she could think of anything else.

Eight

Gaining access to the Ventura family estate hadn't been as difficult as Scarlett feared.

She'd watched the Beverly Hills home for a day, to acquaint herself with the various entrances and to watch who went in and out of the property. There was a guard at the gate that led to a handful of exclusive homes, but getting past him was the easy part since she'd noticed he didn't ring through to the owners for service deliveries. So she'd bought a box of organic produce and claimed she was delivering it to a house at one end of the street. Sure enough, the guard waved her through the gate, and she went to the Ventura home instead.

There, she only had to wheedle her way past an

elderly gardener, who gladly opened another gate for her when he saw her fake delivery. She might have regretted taking advantage of the older man's kindness if she wasn't so thoroughly convinced her mission was just. The Ventura family had done something to alienate Scarlett's mother when Paige—Eden—was just a teen.

Scarlett wasn't leaving until she discovered the truth.

Now, as she lugged two hemp bags full of apples, peaches and Valencia oranges toward the delivery entrance of the expansive French chateau–style home, she wished she had a hand free to text Logan and let him know she'd made it this far. He hadn't wanted her to enter the property alone, but as a rising star in Hollywood, Logan was too well known to sneak in anywhere.

Besides, she didn't want him to compromise his standing with the director of *Winning the West*. Not that he seemed to care what Antonio Ventura thought of him. Ever since the director had held Logan's phone captive on a movie set in the Congo, preventing Logan from messaging Scarlett for weeks, he had no use for the critically acclaimed film guru, even though he was the director of Logan's current movie.

Which, she had to admit, she really liked. She'd been so hurt when she thought Logan had ghosted her. But ever since they'd reconnected, things were looking up. At least, with her relationship. But now her family—her family *name*—was in jeopardy.

Before she could step up to ring the bell on the delivery entrance—which consisted of ornate double doors slightly hidden by a magnolia tree—Scarlett heard a tuneful whistle from the side yard. Curious, she peered through a gap in the boxwood hedge into the European gardens full of paths, statues and fountains. At the far end of the property, a raised gazebo housed a well-dressed older man with his back turned to her.

The gray-haired occupant of the garden pavilion stood at an easel, a paintbrush in hand as he carefully shaded purple flowers with dark smudges on the canvas. Something about his bearing, or maybe it was the perfectly tailored blue shirt with cuffs perfectly turned up, announced his wealth and status. This was no servant. She'd bet her last dollar that the serene painter in the manicured gardens was the owner of the house.

Emilio Ventura, Antonio's adopted father.

Scarlett's biological grandfather.

Emotions sideswiped her like a rogue wave. Anger and resentment topped the list, total indignation that this man had done nothing to reach out to his daughter in a quarter of a decade.

"Excuse me," she called, marching toward him with a sense of righteous purpose. "Mr. Ventura?"

She was halfway across the central courtyard of the elaborate gardens, a wood nymph fountain blowing water through a shell beside her, when the man stopped painting. He slowly turned toward her.

He didn't seem surprised, or worried. He seemed to silently take her measure before he settled his brush in a clear glass container on the tray in front of the easel. Then, as she continued to charge toward him, he picked up a piece of white linen and wiped his hands on it, taking extra time to clean around his nails.

The action only served to provoke her more. Surely she wasn't related to this fastidious old bon vivant living in an ostentatious mansion, too full of himself to care about anyone else? She strode faster, ready to give him a piece of her mind.

"Do you know who I am?" she asked, arriving in his shaded gazebo at last, only to realize she'd brought her organic grocery bags with her for the confrontation.

She set them down a little too quickly, spilling a few Valencia oranges. They rolled along the cool marble floor, one of them landing right in front of his Italian leather loafer.

He stared down at it in bemusement, his bushy eyebrows lifted in surprise.

"I have a general idea," he answered as he bent to retrieve the orange, inspecting it as he straightened again.

Before she could reply, he peered behind her, giving an angry flick of his wrist, seeming to gesture to someone else. Turning, she saw the security guard from the front gate in a golf cart. He was parked on the lawn, speaking to a young woman dressed in a sharp red business suit, her hair piled on her head in an efficient chignon. The woman apparently knew how to interpret Ventura's wrist flick, and she returned to her conversation with the guard.

Scarlett wasn't sure if Emilio had saved her from being thrown off the grounds, or if he'd merely granted her a window of time to speak before they arrested her for trespassing. Either way, she couldn't afford to waste this opportunity to find out why her mother had moved away from home, changed her name and never gone back.

"You have an *idea*." Scarlett crossed her arms and stared him down. "It strikes me as a sad commentary on your parenting when you only have a general idea of your grandchild. In fact, it makes me question why someone like you should have children in the first place if your only role in their lives is donating genetic material."

He flinched just the smallest bit at those last words. He set the orange on his easel and lifted sad, dark eyes toward her. "Did she say that?"

"Who? Did who say that?" Scarlett still didn't regret the tirade, especially as she couldn't detect the least hint of remorse in his expression.

"Your mother," he ventured, shoving his hands in the pockets of his neatly pressed khaki trousers. "My daughter. Because even though you're taking me to task for not knowing my own grandchild, I certainly see my daughter's face reborn in yours."

There was something kind in the way he said it.

Something that, for a moment, made her regret all the times she'd silently wished she looked more like her siblings, who favored the McNeills.

Quickly, she brushed aside any softening of her feelings toward him.

"I can't help but think a man who had treated his daughter with any kindness wouldn't need to guess at her grown child's identity." Scarlett glanced over her shoulder again, wondering if the security guard was on his way over. But the golf cart was nowhere in sight now. "But maybe you plan to have me thrown off the grounds. Is that what you did to my mom all those years ago? Is that why she's never mentioned you? Never visited? Changed her name and hid from you on a Wyoming ranch?"

The older man shook his head, the lines in his face deepening as he frowned. "Never. Eden's mother... Barbara Harris. Have you met her?"

Scarlett shook her head, curious.

"She was a mixed-up girl long before your mother was born," he explained, steepling his fingers together as he walked a slow circle behind the easel. "I loved her deeply, but she wanted no part of a traditional relationship. She was a flower child, I suppose. Full of idealistic dreams that I loved, but she fell into drug use soon after Eden was born. We broke up and I should have taken legal custody of our daughter, but at the time—men didn't do that." He glanced up from his pensive pacing, stopping as if to gauge Scarlett's reaction. "I thought I was doing the right thing to support her decision to live with her mother. I thought she would have extra help. And that worked out okay for a while, until Eden was in middle school and Barbara ran away for months."

Scarlett was drawn in by the family history she never knew, and never even imagined until the scandal broke. She didn't know what to make of her reception, and she still wasn't sure if she was about to be kicked off the property, but she wanted to hear more about her mother's mysterious past.

And as much as she dreaded cutting Emilio any slack, she couldn't deny a strange fascination with watching him as he paced. Seeing him in person and not just in pictures online revealed the likeness to her mother even more. In the way he tilted his head. The turn of a phrase.

"By then, I had married Stella, and I had adopted her son, Antonio. But I told Stella we needed to take Eden in, give her a stable home since her grandmother couldn't watch her all the time. For a few years, it was wonderful having my daughter under my roof. We were a real family." He started pacing again, tipping his chin down to the tips of his fingers. Around them, birds chirped and the fountain babbled musically in the idyllic garden.

Scarlett's stomach knotted, knowing this story didn't have a happy ending. "So what happened?"

"I came home from a long location shoot and Stella said Barbara had returned to take Eden to live with her. I wasn't surprised that it was sudden, or that

Eden didn't come back to visit for the first year or so—that's the way Barbara is. I assumed they were traveling. By the time I saw Barbara again, two years after that, she was back to using, worse off than ever, and couldn't tell me anything about Eden."

Scarlett waited for more. When he said nothing, continuing to walk in circles, a fresh surge of frustration simmered.

"And that's it? You figured your daughter was gone so why bother looking for her? It's fine if she never wants to see you again after you—supposedly—did nothing wrong?" It made no sense to her, and she could see in his face that he fully appreciated that it was illogical.

"I did look for her," he protested. "A little. I asked some journalist friends to use their sources." He quit pacing. "But you're right. I always feared she had a reason for leaving."

"Like?" She gestured with her hands, making a speed-it-up motion, tired of him circling the truth the way he was pacing the gazebo. "You've obviously worked hard to give the world the impression you're living in paradise. Is life in Chateau Ventura not all you've painted it to be?"

Emilio heaved a gusty sigh, his gaze moving toward the easel where his canvas rested. The half-finished painting was of green creeping vines and bougainvillea, with the house in the distance.

"Your mother didn't care for Antonio. I wondered if he had… I don't know. Bullied her in some way." Emilio continued to speak, saying something about his wife being defensive of the boy, but Scarlett couldn't focus on what he was saying.

The pieces shifted in her brain, forming a new picture.

Had her mother run from the son, not the father?

And who was keeping Paige McNeill safe from him now that Antonio was shooting a movie in her mother's backyard? Fear for her mother coiled in her belly.

"I have to leave." She withdrew her cell phone from her pocket, dialing Logan's number. "I need to go home."

Grateful to be back at work, Brock stood outside the training yard, watching his top trainer work with a new two-year-old.

The trainer had messaged him about three of the new horses slated as prospects for competition cutting—a sport designed to show a horse's ability to handle cattle. Brock appreciated the guy's input, especially since the evaluation process was far from scientific, even for the most veteran of equestrian judges. The Creek Spill was gaining a reputation for producing winners, with a core group of elite broodmares. Their breeding program had given Brock the financial security to expand their on-site training, something he personally enjoyed.

Here, at the rail watching an afternoon workout, Brock felt almost like himself. He could forget about the amnesia for a few minutes at a time. Pretend things were normal.

He couldn't say the same for Hannah, however. The woman was firmly on his mind every moment, distracting him with thoughts of the kiss they'd shared the night before. She had surprised the hell out of him when she'd wrapped herself around him. Especially after the way she'd tried to run into the house on her own, without so much as a good-night.

My speed has to do with me trying to outrun my own desires, Brock. Not you...

Her words had floated around in his brain all night, giving him red-hot dreams starring her. Them.

He wouldn't press her about another date, let alone a trip to the West Coast with him. But he couldn't deny that he wanted her. It didn't make sense that he hungered for her this way when he still had the feeling that she was hiding something. His amnesia might leave him cloudy on the last six months, but he had a crystal-clear memory of waking up after the head injury and seeing those shadows in her eyes. Hesitation.

Almost as if she were weighing how much to share.

Pulling out his phone, he typed in a few notes about the two-year-old before he forgot what he wanted to say. He had to agree with the trainer on this one. The horse didn't show enough interest in the cow, while the best cutters usually started with a strong reaction—fear or aggression. Either end of the spectrum could be trained well for cutting, but the horses who were more blasé about the cow required more training and might never have the necessary instincts to make a competitive cutting horse.

The notes helped take his mind off his concerns about Hannah. He'd been with a deceptive woman once before. A woman who'd fed him small lies that might have been forgivable in themselves. Like the time she told him that they shared a mutual acquaintance and later he found out his friend had never met her. Or when she said she loved horses, and it became clear she'd never been around the animals in her life. One of his friends had suggested he should be flattered that Clarice had tried so hard to get close to him. But she hadn't been trying to get close to *him*.

She'd simply wanted to be a McNeill.

The truth had been agonizingly clear when he confronted her on the inconsistencies in the things she said. Brock had realized he had no idea who she really was at all since she'd shown him only a fictional side of herself, a made-up facade intended to appeal to him. It unnerved him to think how well that had worked—and what it said about him.

"Brock," a man called to him from the barn.

Turning, he saw his father ambling over, dressed in worn denim and a T-shirt with the ranch logo. Donovan McNeill had taught his kids that hard work and loyalty earned respect. Not a bank account. He walked the walk, too. Because although he'd been born into wealth and privilege, he'd cut himself off from his father after a dispute over land, and had gone on to become a self-made rancher through relentless work and sheer will.

"Everything okay at home?" Brock asked, instantly on alert. He hadn't seen his dad outside the house since the scandal broke. "How's Paige?"

"She's doing better." Donovan's gaze moved to the training rink where the two-year-old was doing his best to follow the rider's commands. The animal would make a good ranch horse, displaying a willingness to work. "How's the training coming?"

It occurred to Brock that his dad probably appreciated the distraction of ranch duties today as much as him.

Briefly, Brock outlined the trainer's concerns. Donovan had never taken much interest in the quarter horse breeding program until it began turning a profit, letting Brock run with the idea. But in the last year—at least, in the time he remembered—his dad had asked more questions. He'd pushed Brock to develop the training side to grow the business even more.

"You're doing well," his father acknowledged after Brock's explanation, words that counted as glowing praise considering the source. "I left Paige with Madeline for a little while so I could touch base with you and your brothers."

"We would have come to the house—"

Donovan waved off his concern. "Of course. But I got the impression Paige needed a break from all the family living room meetings." Squinting into the sun, his father tipped his head back, lifting the brim of his Stetson to feel the breeze. "I think she feels responsible for the recent spate of news stories, even though I told her it's not her fault."

Brock watched the handler release the cow close to the horse again. "Scarlett puts the blame on us for not trying to work with the blackmailer."

"And she has a damn good point." Donovan jammed his hat back on his head and settled a foot on the rail of the training fence. "Did you hear she waltzed right onto the Ventura estate and confronted Paige's father? Asked the old man what he did to scare off her mother?"

"She's lucky he didn't have her arrested."

Donovan laughed. "How could he? She's his family." His expression turned serious again. "Scarlett seems to think it wasn't Paige's father who made her run, but the son. That damned director we have living right under our roof at the Creek Spill."

"Antonio?" Brock tensed. He couldn't remember meeting the guy personally, but the picture Hannah had painted for him about that encounter told him enough. "We need to get that film crew out of here."

"Except that would be another PR nightmare, according to that publicist we hired. She's recommending we allow the filming to continue so we don't attract even more of a media circus." Donovan scowled. "In the meantime, our investigator has added an extra security detail around my house so Paige is protected."

"And what about the blackmailer?" Brock hadn't heard any more about that since the day of his accident when Carson's girlfriend had shared her fears that her unstable mother was behind the whole thing. "Has the investigator looked into that angle?"

"He says he's got multiple people working on it. He doesn't have enough evidence to contact the police for an arrest, but apparently Jane Layton had a lot of access to the Ventura family in her years as their maid."

Brock listened, but his brain was still stuck on Antonio Ventura possibly being the reason his stepmother had left home as a teen. He didn't like the idea of Hannah working for someone like that. Brock wondered if he approached Paige himself and shared his fears for Hannah whether he might have better luck getting his stepmother to share something concrete about her past.

"In the meantime," his father continued, "Maisie said Scarlett is coming home. At least for the duration of the filming since her new boyfriend is an actor in the thing."

"That's good." He didn't hold out hope they could convince his half sister to stick around the ranch afterward, though. "I think we'd all feel better if we could part on better terms with her. At least help her see the family's side of the decision not to negotiate with the blackmailer."

Donovan nodded. "That girl has more grit than anyone I know. I hoped if I kept her on the ranch long enough, she'd find a role for herself. Decide to stay here after all."

"She always wanted to be an actress," Brock pointed out, gesturing to the trainer that he'd seen enough with the two-year-old in the pen. As long as he was here, he might as well view the other animals.

"And I hoped it was a phase." Donovan shrugged, then pounded his fist on the top rail. "But maybe she's going to need that acting career if she's not even a legal McNeill."

Brock noted the set to his father's jaw. The cold anger in his eyes. "Dad, you know we'd never deny the girls their inheritance."

"I'm telling you what the lawyers explained to me. There's no fast way to sort out all the paperwork that details what they're entitled to." His voice had a dry, rough tone, hinting at emotions that Brock almost never saw in him. "Without the McNeill name to protect them, they could lose out on more than just the ranches." He shot Brock a level gaze. "If Malcolm died tomorrow, they'd get nothing from his estate. And I have blamed my father for a lot, but that wouldn't be any fault of his. It's on me for not knowing my marriage wasn't legal."

"How do we fix it?" Brock asked, understanding better now. McNeill Resorts was a global corporation with a net worth that far outstripped the ranches. But even then, it wasn't about the money. It was about the name. Family. Legacy. Future generations.

Because even when Donovan had cut himself off

from his father, he'd kept the name, and he'd placed value on it.

"For starters, I've got to marry Paige again." Straightening from the rail, Donovan squared his shoulders. "She has been through too much already to give her just some quickie date with a judge to make us legal. As soon as I can pull the pieces together to make it special, there's going to be a wedding at the Black Creek Ranch."

A wedding.

Brock could tell by the tone of his father's voice that he was counting the hours until he could make it happen. Did that mean tomorrow? The next day?

As his father turned on his heel, Brock guessed that Donovan was on his way to deliver the news to the rest of the family. Or maybe to shop for a new ring. Brock was seeing a more sentimental side of his dad this week, that was for sure.

For his own part, Brock already knew who he was going to ask to be his date. The trip to the West Coast might not be happening with Hannah anytime soon, but he couldn't think of anyone else he'd want at his side when his father said his vows.

Nine

"He invited you to go to a *wedding* with him?" Callie asked Hannah as they stood together in one of the wardrobe trailers.

"Shh." Hannah didn't want the word to get around the set that Paige and Donovan were getting married for a second time. She peered over her shoulder through the open door where she could see an animal handler walking past with one of the horses that specialized in tricks. "It's got to stay between you and me, okay?"

Brock had phoned the night before to ask her if she could be ready within a few hours' notice to attend a secret family wedding, tonight or tomorrow. She had tried to tell herself it would give her a perfect pretext to speak privately with Callie—she could ask to borrow a dress and then try to find out more about why she'd used the word "lewd" to describe Antonio. But instead of coming up with ways to convince Callie to confide in her, Hannah had fallen asleep thinking about how a dance at a wedding reception would put her in Brock's arms again.

As much as she'd like to think the attraction was all just sensual chemistry, she knew better. Every moment spent with Brock McNeill made her like him more. And made her regret the barrier she'd put between them that would ensure he would regret this relationship when his memory returned. She'd done it to keep herself from falling for a man like her father, like the sailor who lashed himself to the mast to keep from following the siren's song. It seemed so smart at the time, but when temptation called…

"Why the secrecy?" Callie asked, glancing up from the rolling rack where she was tucking a lace sleeve back into a garment bag.

"They won't want any media attention." Hannah hoped she hadn't made a mistake trusting her friend. "I don't want to be the one to ruin their wedding after all they've been through."

"Right." Straightening, Callie thumbed through more hangers, looking over the options for Hannah. "I forget this isn't Hollywood where everyone *says* they don't want media attention, when they actually crave it like their next hit." She pulled out a blue lace skirt. "What about this? I brought it by mistake. You could wear it with a silk tank and dress it up."

"Maybe." Hannah could already feel Brock's hands on her waist where the two fabrics might meet. Where a thumb might accidentally brush along bare skin. Shaking off the imaginings, she focused on why she really came to the wardrobe trailer after her time on set. "Callie, I have a question. About… Antonio."

She lowered her voice when she said his name. Then for good measure, she turned and closed the trailer door. They were the only ones inside. Callie stared at her curiously.

"What is it?"

"Do you remember when you told me about the photo someone posted with the 'separated at birth' caption?" At her nod, Hannah pressed on, hoping she hadn't misunderstood the woman's previous comment. "You used the word 'lewd' to describe him."

Callie's face flushed. She looked confused. Betrayed, even. "Did I?" Her hands slid away from the hangers and she folded her arms across her chest. "I'm not sure what you're getting at."

Flustered, Hannah rushed to reassure her. "I'm not getting at anything. And I don't mean to be nosy, I just… I've heard things about him. And I wondered—"

"I haven't heard anything." Callie shook her head, her eyes bright with emotion, her shoulders tense.

"And I think you made a mistake about what I said. Everyone is so quick to judge."

"I'm not judging—"

"Hannah, I think you'd better go, okay? I won't tell anyone about the wedding, but this is a conversation I'm not comfortable having." She thrust the blue lace skirt into Hannah's hands and stalked into the trailer's tiny bathroom, locking the door with a *click* behind her.

Did that seem like the response of a woman who didn't know anything about Antonio's behavior? Unsure how to proceed without alienating a potential ally for Hope, Hannah walked toward the closed door. She paused outside, and said softly, "I'm leaving, but I want you to know you can talk to me if you change your mind. I didn't mean to upset you."

When there was no reply, Hannah walked out of the trailer, leaving the lace skirt behind. She didn't want Callie to think she was trying to take advantage of her. Maybe she shouldn't have used the pretense of borrowing a dress as a reason to come here at an off time.

But far from being discouraged about what she'd discovered, Hannah hoped she was on to something. Maybe after Callie had time to think it over, she would decide to confide in Hannah.

Until then, she had a secret wedding to prepare for.

Brock rode home late that night, urging Aurora faster after a long evening working with his brothers to turn an empty barn on the Black Creek Ranch into a wedding venue. The barn they'd cleaned was old and unused, but it was structurally sound with plenty of picturesque appeal. His father didn't want to hire too many outsiders to help prepare for the wedding in an effort to keep the ceremony out of the media, so Brock had pitched in with Carson and Cody to get the space in shape.

Working with his brothers had felt like old times. Especially since the barn dated from the days when the Calderon family had owned the land, before Donovan had married Kara Calderon, Brock's mother. Brock had mixed memories growing up on the Black Creek Ranch, some happy, some—like his mother's death—gut-wrenching. He'd been only three at the time, but his earliest memories were from that day. Flashes of ambulance lights. His father falling to his knees.

But life had gone on at the main house after his mother's death. Paige had joined their lives, becoming a nanny and then, Donovan's new wife. Yet somehow, she'd never really been "Mom." She'd always been quiet. Unassuming. A steady presence in their home while their father charged in and out, his bigger personality the driving force of the McNeills.

It occurred to Brock that while Scarlett favored their mother in looks, she was more like Donovan in personality—someone you noticed immediately. Whereas Madeline, the oldest of the girls, took after Paige, quietly attending to business while running the

White Canyon Ranch, a guest ranch where many of the cast members of *Winning the West* were staying.

Guiding Aurora toward home, Brock slowed the mare as he neared Hannah's cabin. He had planned to drop off some things she might need for the wedding earlier, but missed an opportunity when his father asked for help at the barn. He'd had one of the ranch hands deliver the packages instead. Now, it was almost midnight, but the cabin lamps blazed and another opera aria floated on the breeze through an open window. Clearly she was still awake. Besides, the Perseid meteor shower was peaking this week, lighting up the sky with streaking stars.

How could he let her miss it?

Reining in, he dropped down to the ground and then climbed the steps onto the porch. Before he knocked, however, he pulled out his phone to text her so she'd know who was at the door. Through the open window, he could hear her phone chime and, a moment later, a soft laugh.

Then, footsteps.

Anticipation speared straight through him.

When the door opened, Hannah was dressed in a worn purple T-shirt that said But First… Coffee, and a pair of cotton pajama pants in bright blue. Her hair was woven in a messy braid, her face scrubbed clean. With no makeup, she was even prettier. There was nothing to detract from her wise gray eyes and expressive mouth.

"This is getting to be a habit, Cowboy," she

drawled, stepping out onto the welcome mat to look over his shoulder. "What will the neighbors say?"

He caught a hint of her shampoo as she stood by him. He battled a fierce urge to lean down and breathe in the scent of her.

"Since there's no one around for almost a mile, I think we're okay." He gestured to his horse. "And Aurora doesn't judge."

"No?" A smile curved her lips. "Then no wonder you chose a career where you're surrounded by horses."

He heard the edge in her voice and wondered if he'd struck a nerve.

"You're in a notoriously competitive field," he said carefully, waving her outside. "And I won't stay long. I only came to show you something out here."

"Outside in the dark?" she asked, her voice full of skepticism.

"Yes, ma'am. Grab a sweater if you want. Or shoes. But you can see it from the deck."

"It's the least I can do, since I owe you a thank-you for the surprise packages you had sent over here today." She leaned to one side, pulling a gray cardigan sweater off a hat rack made of elk antlers by the door. "I was stunned to find a few options for dresses to wear to the wedding."

"It was my pleasure since you were kind enough to be my date on short notice." He tugged the lightweight cashmere from her hands. "Allow me."

He held the shoulders wide so she could slide one arm in, and then the other.

Releasing the collar, he let the fabric fall against her neck. Then, unable to resist, he slipped his hand beneath the braid trapped by the material, tugging it free. Her hair was soft as silk on his skin.

His hand faltered in midair, his brain reeling at how much he wanted to keep on touching her.

"It was very thoughtful of you. Thank you." She edged away quickly, stepping out the door and onto the welcome mat after sliding sandals on her feet. He noticed that her toenails were painted bright pink. "I'm ready."

He took her hand, telling himself it was for practical purposes since he didn't want her to trip in the dark. "Be careful."

Brock wanted to get closer to her. To learn more about her. See if he could unlock the secrets in her eyes.

Failing that, he just wanted to spend time with her. To lose himself in the warmth of her smile. The ease of being with someone who didn't want to talk about blackmail and PR strategies. Hell, he just wanted to enjoy the simple pleasure of stargazing with her.

The opera that was playing ended, giving way to a more haunting melody, the sound growing quieter as he led her to the darker back corner of the deck for the best view.

"Close your eyes." He spoke the words softly, against her hair, his jaw against her temple.

"You're being very mysterious," she accused softly. "I can hardly see in front of me as it is."

"Just trust me." He let go of her hand to cover her eyes with one hand, his arm around her. She felt so right against him, like she belonged there.

But he didn't let himself get distracted by that now. He tipped her head back.

"You can open now." He moved his hand away, staring up into the night sky with her as a streak of light grazed the heavens above their heads.

She gasped with delight, her face full of wonder in the pale glow of the waning moon. "How did you know that would happen?"

"I didn't. That was just good timing." He pulled over a cushioned patio bench for her. "It's the peak of the Perseid meteor shower this week. I thought maybe you'd enjoy one of the benefits of living far from city lights. Our views are usually really good out here."

"That's amazing." Her eyes continued to scan the skies even as she took a seat. "Should I turn off the light inside?"

"I can get it." He jogged around to the front of the house again, reaching inside the front door long enough to flip the main switch before rejoining her.

He dropped onto the bench next to her, tossing aside an extra pillow to make more room for himself. He slid off his hat and set it on the planked floor while the opera ladies sang back and forth on the music still playing inside.

"Look!" Hannah pointed overhead to a streak of green, white and red. "I don't think I've ever seen a shooting star before."

"It's comet rubble, I think. Earth passes through the orbital path of a comet this time of year, so the streaks are bits of cosmic debris hitting the atmosphere."

"'Shooting star' has a more poetic ring to it." She kept her gaze fixed on the sky. "I hope your father and stepmother are watching. It seems like a good omen for the night before their wedding."

"They've got a lock on all things romantic for tomorrow," he assured her. "I just finished clearing out the barn with my brothers, and my sisters were starting to decorate when we left. Madeline showed me a photo of what they're going for and it should look really nice."

"They're decorating now? At almost midnight?" She glanced over at him. "I'm surprised the McNeill family doesn't have a fleet of workers to do things like that for them."

"Dad has always stressed the value of hard work. But even if he wanted to hire out the jobs, his hands are tied this week since he doesn't want to attract any extra attention to the ranch or invite media speculation."

"So this will be a low-key event?"

"Not in the slightest." He spotted the start of another meteor and pointed toward the arc of white light. Here in the shadow of the house with a wide-open view of the night sky, they had the best possible seat for the event. "My father is determined that Paige feel the full love and support of the family tomorrow, so he's doing everything in his power to make it memorable."

"Such as?" Hannah slid off a shoe and tucked one foot under her. Her knee brushed against his thigh and rogue visions swamped him. Passionate visions that he needed to lock down fast.

He dragged in a deep, cooling breath of night air and kept his eyes on the stars.

"I don't want to ruin any of the surprises. But he's having services like the catering truck come through the gates at three in the morning in an effort to elude media interest." Brock had to hand it to the old man. He'd planned carefully.

"Very smart of him." Hannah clutched his knee as another meteor streaked past in a blue blaze. "The colors are so pretty."

Brock's pulse slugged harder as he began to doubt the wisdom of inviting her out here. He wanted to get to know her better, but it wasn't easy to make friendly chitchat when the attraction rocketed between them hotter than any fiery cosmic debris.

He closed his eyes for a second, trying to stay in the moment and the conversation. Trying to remember he was here to get to know her better, not test the heat of their chemistry.

"I'm happily surprised at the level of effort Dad has made. My stepmother has been the unsung rock of our family for as long as they've been married, and I'm glad he's recognizing that."

Hannah gave a bitter laugh. "Some men go a lifetime without noticing the good people in their lives. My father walked out on Mom, Hope and me the moment he found a woman whose ambitions matched his own."

"I'm sorry you went through that." He plucked up the end of her braid where it sat on her shoulder, testing the ends against his finger. "And even though that was extremely wrong of him, I wonder if it wasn't easier on your mother than if she had stayed another fifteen years with a man who didn't appreciate her enough."

Had Paige stayed with his father only because she felt trapped? Because she was hiding from her real family, using the protection of the McNeill name?

"Maybe it was," Hannah admitted. "But he sure didn't do Hope any favors by writing her off."

"What about you, Hannah?" Brock set down her braid, easing forward on the bench to see her expression now that his eyes were accustomed to the dark. "It had to be equally difficult for you."

"No." She shook her head, vehemence in her voice. "I don't need someone who puts more value on material things than people. But my sister was young enough when he left that I think it made her more... susceptible to the promise of love and acceptance."

"Susceptible?" He wanted to learn more about her, and he'd sure latched on to something tonight, but he couldn't quite identify what it was. Resentment, yes. But Brock felt like he was only getting half the story. "You make love and acceptance sound like an illness."

"It can be when you seek it too desperately because you weren't given enough as a child." Anger tightened her voice. "It makes you a target for people to take advantage of you."

He turned that over for a long moment, thinking through the implications of the little she'd shared. The night sky gave them something to focus on so the silence didn't feel awkward. Finally, he broke the quiet.

"It sounds like Hope has been through a lot." He slid his palm over to where Hannah's rested on the cushion between them. Slipping his fingers between each of hers, he squeezed her hand. "But she obviously has a fierce protector in you, Hannah. You were probably better for her than any inattentive father could have been."

For a long moment, he simply felt her pulse gently drumming in the heel of her hand beneath her thumb. But eventually, she turned her gaze toward him.

"I would gladly trade my own happiness for hers." She spoke with a conviction that made it sound like she'd already made that devil's bargain. "But I'm not sure that it will do her any good."

Brock couldn't add up the pieces of her cryptic confidences. Maybe it was because of the amnesia, and his brain was only working at half speed. Or maybe it was because the attraction thwarted his more noble intentions. But selfishly, he wished he could ease that hurt in her eyes.

"You can't live your life for someone else. Or give away your happiness to save another person's." His free hand found the soft curve of her cheek, his thumb stroking her there. "It doesn't work like that."

Her eyes fluttered as he touched her. Out here, under the natural fireworks of the night sky, it felt like they were all alone on the edge of the world, with no witnesses except the night breeze to hear them.

He caught himself moving toward her. Knew he needed to hold back.

"I haven't given *all* my happiness away," she admitted, opening her eyes wide again, her pupils dilated so that there was only the slimmest gray ring around the edges. "I could still have one taste."

Her gaze dipped to his mouth, torching his restraint.

"One kiss. That's all," he swore…to himself? To her? To the universe?

He didn't know.

Gently, he angled her chin up and captured her lips with his. Heat spiked in his spine, tightening his shoulders and tensing everything else. She melted into him, her lips parting, back arching, molding delectable feminine curves against him.

He untwined their fingers because he needed both hands on her to steady her hips. To still her for a moment. Ensure she didn't end up in his lap. Because if that happened...

"Brock." She breathed his name against his damp mouth as her fingers raked down his back and up again.

She wriggled closer, the heat of her skin warming his palms right through the thick fabric of the pajama bottoms.

Ah, damn.

He hauled her across his thighs, knowing they couldn't take this any further outside under the stars. She straddled him, her knees locked against his waist, the heat of her sex evident right through the denim of his fly.

Things could go off the rails so fast if he wasn't careful.

Especially since he could feel her heart pounding, and the soft moans she made when she kissed him were the sweetest sounds he'd ever heard.

But there was something fragile inside Hannah Ryder. Some secret or some hurt, he didn't know which anymore, that kept her from him. So he was going to honor that "one kiss" vow if it killed him.

And pulling away from her, his breathing more ragged than if he'd run the perimeter of the ranch, he thought it just might.

"I want you," he told her simply, their breathing slowing as they stared at each other in the moonlight. Stars winked behind her, meteors streaking the sky like the world was about to end. "But only when you're sure." He slid her to the bench seat beside him, knowing he needed to leave before he broke the promise he wanted to keep. He pressed a kiss to her temple before standing. "Only when you're ready."

Walking away wasn't easy with her sigh of regret whispering on the wind, even knowing she'd be on his arm tomorrow at the wedding.

Ten

Hannah picked a stray piece of straw from the hem of her silk organza dress. She never would have guessed the first surprise of the wedding day would be arriving at the ceremony in a hay wagon pulled by a big green John Deere.

She'd heard the tractor rumbling closer late in the afternoon when she had been expecting to see Brock. Instead of her date, a boy dressed in a cowboy hat and overalls—boutonniere pinned to the denim strap—knocked on her door and invited her into the wagon. One of the ranch hands had rolled out a carpet for her so she didn't ruin her shoes, and when she'd stepped up into the unlikely conveyance, she'd been greeted by a handful of other guests, including

Carson McNeill's girlfriend, the stuntwoman Emma Layton, and Cody's pregnant fiancée, Jillian Ross, the woman who'd been the location scout for *Winning the West*. Jillian, a gorgeous redhead dressed in a bright green-and-yellow tulle dress, explained that the men were helping their father get ready for the wedding, but that Brock had wanted to make sure Hannah had family to keep her company until he could join her at the ceremony.

Now, as the wagon bumped over a ravine close to the Black Creek Ranch, Hannah held on to one of the hay bales strapped to the sides. They were piled high on the exterior of the wagon to help shield wedding guests from long lens cameras and drones since the McNeills were trying to keep the tabloids from ruining their day.

Hannah feared she was going to end up ruining the day for Brock in the end anyhow. She couldn't sleep after he left the night before, regretting that she hadn't come clean with him about what they'd shared that first night together. She couldn't deny that she had feelings for him, a fact pounded home by the way his kiss had dominated her dreams in the fitful hours when she had finally closed her eyes.

She hadn't been honest about their heated first encounter because she'd been consumed with worry about her sister and hatred for Antonio. And when she'd first learned Brock was a McNeill, she'd been floored by the idea that she'd slept with a man related to Antonio Ventura—if only on paper.

Now that she knew Brock better, understood him for the kind of man he was inside, she owed him the truth. After the wedding festivities tonight, she would tell him. He'd been through so much with his family this week it didn't seem fair to ruin his day. She wanted him to celebrate his father's wedding. But her conscience wouldn't let her enjoy another one of those toe-curling kisses without telling him the truth.

And then, it would be over.

So she planned to savor this day as much as she could before she offered her heart up for Brock to break.

"Your dress is beautiful, Hannah," Emma was saying to her. A brunette with wide, dark eyes and delicate features, she wore a simply cut navy sheath. "And you look so familiar to me, I feel like we've met before."

Tensing, Hannah knew her time of reckoning would come with this family. She just hadn't wanted it to be today. At least, not yet.

Hannah forced a smile, reminding herself all the subterfuge had been for a good cause. "Now that you mention it, you look familiar to me, too. I think we worked for the same temp agency last spring."

Emma frowned for a moment, then snapped her fingers. "Yes! I remember. We shared a house clean-ing assignment one day in Beverly Hills, didn't we?"

Thankfully, it hadn't been the Ventura house

when they'd worked together, which would have been a little too close for comfort.

The tractor downshifted, the engine noise quieting a bit as they slowed their progress. Around them, a few of the other guests took group selfies, posing with wildflowers that one of them had picked on a stop to load more guests.

"We do what we need to in order to make ends meet between jobs," Hannah replied before redirecting the conversation. "How have you enjoyed the stunt work on this film?"

"I've grown really attached to the horses," she admitted, graciously taking the bait. "And I don't know how I would have gotten through the shoot without Carson, and now, his whole family." She lowered her voice so that only Jillian and Hannah could hear. "I know in my gut now that my mother has been the one behind the blackmail. But we have to wait for the private investigator to have enough evidence before they will—" Emma blinked fast and whispered "—*arrest* her."

Jillian slipped a supportive arm around the woman, quietly murmuring something to her.

"I'm so sorry," Hannah said, meaning every word. She stood up enough to drag her hay bale seat in front of Emma, shielding her from view of the rest of the wagon to hide the other woman's tears. "I had no idea."

Jillian dug in her purse for a tissue and passed it to her friend while focusing on Hannah. "We know

Brock has been dealing with a lot, with losing some of his memory. How is he feeling?"

Guilt gnawed at Hannah. She'd been so focused on her own family problems while Brock's had been going through hell this week. "His head doesn't ache anymore, but I know it frustrates him that he can't remember the last several months."

Emma halted in the middle of wiping her eyes. "I don't think he even recognized me when he saw me at Donovan's earlier this week."

Hannah nodded. "I know the dynamics of the scandal have been confusing for him since he doesn't remember everything leading up to it." She bit her lip, wondering if she should ask them the question that Brock couldn't help her with now that he had amnesia. The question that had kept her from telling Brock the truth when he woke up with no memory. "Do you think the McNeill family knew about Paige's real identity before the scandal broke?"

The wagon rolled to a stop. Violin music played nearby.

Emma shook her head. Jillian blurted, "Cody was blindsided. Completely stunned."

Hannah stood with the other women, unable to enjoy the swell of excitement through the rest of the group as they caught sight of the decorated barn where Donovan and Paige would exchange their vows and host a reception.

She had hidden the truth of that first night from Brock fearing that he could have a loyalty to the

Ventura family. She hadn't expected to fall for the rancher in the meantime. She hadn't thought the omission would ever come back to bite her.

As she stepped down onto the lawn outside the barn, glimpsing Brock in his black tuxedo, his blue eyes locking on her, Hannah could already feel the ache of all she was about to lose.

Scarlett felt like an alien on a foreign planet as the wedding music began.

The people filling the barn were familiar enough, of course. She'd grown up on the Black Creek Ranch, and then after college, she'd moved into a remodeled bunkhouse on the property. She'd played hide-and-seek in this barn with her sisters, and she had once rescued a scared kitten from one of the rafters.

But the barn looked nothing like it had back then, when it was full of rusty old farm equipment. With the highest windows opened to let fresh air in, the barn's gray stone walls were a beautiful backdrop to six-foot-tall candelabra spaced every few feet and decorated with cream-colored ribbons and white flowers. The heavy rafters were polished to gleaming, the wood glowing in the reflection of white fairy lights raining down from the ceiling. White tulle was hung tent-like between the beams.

The whole place smelled like lemon wax and roses. The linen-draped tables were decorated with white freesia and snapdragons in clear glass jars filled with bright yellow lemon slices.

And even the people seemed different. Her brother Brock, who normally never left the horse barn, suddenly couldn't take his eyes off the beautiful actress he was with. And their surly father had developed a solicitousness where his wife was concerned, a tender affection that Scarlett hadn't seen in all her twenty-five years.

She squeezed Logan's hand beside her as they took their seats in the front row on the bride's side. Madeline and her boyfriend, Sawyer, sat in the row with them, Maisie was sandwiched between the two couples and decidedly alone.

"I hardly recognize this place," Scarlett whispered to Maisie. "And am I to really believe Dad went to all of this trouble on his own for Mom?"

Maisie poked her with her elbow, more from sisterly habit than anything. A love poke. Scarlett jabbed her in the arm in return. She'd missed her.

"Do you see these bags under my eyes?" Maisie whispered as the wedding music began. "I was up half the night decorating, thank you very much. But yes, it was all Dad's idea."

"Unbelievable. I'm gone for a week and the whole world turns upside down. Suddenly Dad is a romantic?" She was going to have a hard time staying angry with her father after this. She hadn't seen him since her flight had landed late the night before, but her mother had seemed stronger and surprisingly happy when she'd visited with her this afternoon to help her dress.

Scarlett hadn't had the heart to quiz her mother about Antonio Ventura on the day of her second wedding to their father, but she would. Soon.

"Believe me, it's freaking me out," Maisie whispered behind her hand as they stood for the bride's entrance. "I'll be the only cynic in the family at this rate."

All the McNeill relatives in attendance were paired off, too. Ian and Lydia McNeill had made the flight with patriarch Malcolm and his fiancée, Rose. Lydia was pregnant with their first child and positively glowing. Damon and Caroline McNeill were there, too, taking a break from Transparent, the software company Damon headed in Silicon Valley.

"Even Brock is dating again." Scarlett had seen one of Hannah Ryder's films and thought she was talented but didn't know much about her personally. "I asked Logan if he's ever worked with Hannah before, but he said no."

"Brock has amnesia," Maisie reminded her. "I'm worried about him."

"I'll talk to him," Scarlett said before all eyes turned to her mother at the entrance of the barn.

Paige looked beautiful in a slim ivory gown with a lace shrug that covered her shoulders. Her brown hair fell in glossy curls that Scarlett had talked her into. Normally, her mother favored a ponytail, her part a razor-straight line down the center of her head. But Scarlett had begged for curls and a bow, and her mother had agreed that it was "time for some changes."

Behind Scarlett, Logan leaned close to speak into her ear, sending a delicious shiver down her spine just from his nearness.

"Look at your dad," he said.

Scarlett glanced around Maisie's shoulder where she could see her father's face. The naked emotion there caught her off-guard. Love. Tenderness. A shining pride in the woman who walked toward him. Scarlett gulped back a tear at the same time Maisie dug in her handbag for tissues. She passed two over her shoulder.

As the vows began, Scarlett knew she'd been mistaken when she'd accused her father of being unfeeling about her mother's welfare. Of course, she'd been right about her brothers being too protective when they'd sent a private investigator to LA to keep tabs on her. But she was going to forgive them because they were older brothers, and that was their thing.

Besides, she was empathizing a little too well now that she knew someone from her mother's past had hurt her. All her own protective instincts were roaring.

For now, she was going to enjoy the wedding. Afterward, she would talk to her mother about what had happened in Emilio Ventura's home to make Paige a fugitive from her own family. Because Scarlett wasn't interested in simply weathering a scandal and protecting the McNeill name.

She planned to find out who was responsible for hurting her mom. And then hold them accountable.

Hannah stepped outside the barn just as the dancing started, needing a breath of fresh air.

The chamber musicians who had played earlier were packing up their instruments and loading them into the back of a pickup truck nearby. Inside, a country-western band had started to play, bringing the crowd onto a makeshift dance floor in one corner of the barn. The white lights and candelabra made the whole building glow, illuminating patches of the meadow around it through the open windows and doors.

The summer night had brought a cool breeze with it, and Hannah let the wind blow her silk organza dress, the guilty knot of feelings tightening in her belly the longer this night went on.

Behind her, she heard a familiar male voice. "I've been looking forward to a dance all day."

Heat rushed through her, that jolt of reaction Brock could always elicit. With a word. A look. A touch.

She couldn't deny him this dance. Not when the bride and groom were still celebrating inside.

"Me, too," she told him honestly, taking his hand and letting him lead her back inside.

The band had swapped to a sultry slow song, the singer crooning romantic words that amplified all of the things she was feeling. The longing. The hunger.

The fear that things wouldn't last. As they reached the dance floor crowded with couples, Brock spun her easily into his arms, a protective hand at her waist, holding her close.

"I'm happy for my father," he confided, nodding toward the bride and groom in the middle of the dance floor.

Donovan McNeill had eyes only for his wife as they swayed together. Paige glowed in his attention, her diamond wedding ring glittering in the reflection of a thousand fairy lights as she rested her hand on her husband's shoulder.

"He pulled off an incredible event on very little notice," she agreed. "And I haven't seen any sign of paparazzi lurking."

"So far, so good." Brock's hand shifted on her waist as he stared down at her, his touch making her breath catch. "You look beautiful tonight."

She felt herself falling for him, her defenses crumbling fast. If only this could be real.

"I owe it to you for sending me the gown." The silk organza hem teased against her calf, the delicate material fluttering around her as they moved.

Pale pink and dotted with tiny flowers, the dress was romantic without being too sweet. The cold shoulder treatment of the sleeves gave it a dose of sexy.

"I'm not talking about the gown," he assured her, leaning closer. "It's all you. Thank you for being my date tonight."

She bit her lip, not sure what to say. She just knew she needed to redirect the conversation before she dug them both in deeper.

"It's a testament to your family that you've come together this way, to celebrate a marriage and focus on the positive after all you've been through."

The slow song came to an end, but Brock didn't let go of her.

"I'm going to try to take a page from Dad's playbook and put the past behind me. Not worry about the memories I've lost. Just enjoy the present with you."

All around them, the couples on the dance floor clapped for the band. Hannah could only think about how thoroughly she'd screwed things up with Brock. Before she could say anything, he whispered in her ear.

"I want to go on a real date with you. Away from the family and the ranch. Get to know you." He stared into her eyes, even while the singer announced the bride and groom were getting ready to take their leave.

The movement all around them, the rush to share hugs and good wishes with the couple, saved Hannah from having to answer right away.

Brock took her hand and led her toward the doors so they could see off Donovan and Paige. Hannah knew her time with Brock would come to an end once the couple made their exit. She couldn't accept his offer, not when she hadn't been truthful.

And then after she told him, she knew, he wouldn't be asking for another date.

Turning, she faced Brock. He looked far too tempting in his dark tuxedo, his handsome face bathed in moonlight.

She needed to speak fast before she weakened. Inhaling a bracing breath, she blurted, "Once we're finished here, there's something we need to talk about."

Eleven

Half an hour later, back at her cabin for the night, Hannah invited Brock inside so they could talk.

Nerves wound tight, she knew there was no other way to move forward. She needed to tell Brock the truth about that first night they spent together. Even so, it worried her that she wasn't free to tell him everything. Hope's secret was not Hannah's to share, and her sister's emotional health and well-being had to come before everything else.

No matter how much she wanted to unburden herself fully.

"You look so serious." Brock took her hands in his as they stood in the cabin's tiny foyer. "Let's sit and we'll talk."

He pressed the button on the remote that made the gas fireplace blaze to life. The orange flames leaped silently with no logs to crackle or pop. The warm light cast a romantic glow in the living area as Brock tugged her down to sit beside him on the leather sofa.

She shifted to see his face, knowing there was no easy way to say this.

"I haven't been honest with you." She stared down at her hands, her nails free of any polish because of the time period of the film she was shooting. She toyed with the eternity knot ring she wore, a simple sterling silver piece that matched the one she'd given to her sister for her high school graduation.

Even then, Hannah had known they were each other's best support system.

Brock tensed beside her. She didn't have to see him to know. She could feel it. They were so in tune with each other physically. Would she be losing that with her admission? God, she hoped not.

"How so?"

"It's about that first time we met," she answered. "The night you don't remember because of the amnesia. I didn't tell you everything that happened." She glanced up to see him watching her, his expression neutral.

Was he reserving judgment? She wasn't certain.

"What happened?" he asked, his voice remote and lacking its usual warmth. "What did you leave out?"

Her pulse sped faster.

"I made a split-second decision about not sharing the details when you woke up with no memory. It seemed like the right choice then," she said quickly, needing to explain.

"What have you omitted?" he pressed, and she could hear his patience fracturing. There was a tense frustration threaded through the words.

"We were together that night," she blurted, glancing up to see his reaction. "Intimately."

His eyebrows shot up. But other than that, he showed no reaction, saying nothing for the space of three painfully long heartbeats. She held her breath, waiting.

Then his mouth went tight for a moment and she knew. This wasn't going to go well.

"You took advantage of the amnesia to tell me your own version of events." His voice was level, but there was a flash of emotion in his blue eyes. Anger. Frustration.

Both well deserved.

"I did, and I'm not proud of it." She twisted the ring around her finger, again and again. "That night was my fault. I instigated what happened, and we hadn't even—I didn't even know your name at the time." She still couldn't believe it had happened at all. "I never do things like that. It had been a stressful night, and then we shared a horseback ride over here—that part of what I told you was true."

His jaw flexed as he listened. He did not interrupt.

Instead, he waited. Shadows from the fire danced across his face.

She pulled in a shaky breath, her emotions all over the place. "The closeness and the touching... I don't know how to describe what it did to me. But the shoot had been so hellish that day, and then when we touched—"

"Why?" he demanded, cutting through her confusion and guilt with one simple question.

"Why did things ignite so fast? I don't know, we just—"

"No. Why was the shoot hellish?" he asked more gently. "Because of the director? Because of the long hours in the hay that day?"

She'd told him those details. Had shared everything right up until he'd taken her back to the cabin.

Her thumb traced the silver loops in the eternity knot. She couldn't share the impotent fury she felt every time she looked at Antonio Ventura, let alone took direction from him. She couldn't confide her sister's pain when Hope wanted more than anything to keep her ordeal private.

It tore Hannah up inside, because the secret hurt her, too. But it was a pain she could never share when Hope's was a thousand times greater.

"Yes," Hannah lied, blinking fast and hating herself. "Ventura is mercurial, and the churlishness of his demands make this business far harder than it has to be."

That much was true. But it certainly didn't give

a glimpse of the real torment of her time on location in Cheyenne, the burden of it lightened only by Brock's presence. Her time with him had given her something good to savor in spite of everything ugly around her.

Still, her throat burned, the weight of what she couldn't say weighing down her conscience even as she shared.

"Hannah, look at me." Brock's voice wound around her, his hand sliding over hers in an unexpected touch.

"I didn't tell you about what happened between us because it felt like a second chance for me to… not get so carried away again." Her pulse thrummed faster, nerves knotting with agitation. "I thought if you forgot it, I would, too, and we'd both move on."

"But here we are. Right back where we started that night." His thumb brushed back and forth over her palm.

The tenderness of his touch caught her off guard.

"You should be raging at me for deceiving you all this time." She willed away the flare of heat that came with his caress. "I should have told you the truth."

"Yes. But I can think of a few times in my life that I would have grabbed the chance to rewrite history." The warmth in his voice soothed her soul. "That's forgivable, Hannah."

Not daring to believe her ears, she searched for some sign she may have misunderstood him. But the expression on his face appeared open and honest, his body language open and relaxed.

And hot.

With his bow tie loosened and the top button unfastened on his shirt, he looked enticingly disheveled. His broad shoulders filled out his jacket, the fabric stretching around his biceps as he leaned forward to touch her. His intent was unmistakable.

"Is it truly forgivable?" Her heart skipped a beat.

She hadn't even considered a scenario where Brock would want to pick up where they'd left off. She melted inside a little to think there might still be a way for them to be together.

A future that included a second chance.

"It is. The question I want you to consider is, now that you have a chance to rewrite history, do you still want to forget what we shared ever happened?" He lifted his hand to her face, grazing the back of one knuckle along her jaw. "Or do you want to relive that memory?"

Brock breathed in the scent of her, relishing the way her pupils dilated at his touch. The firelight gave her pale hair a burnished glow, her cheeks even more flushed color.

He could tell she was surprised that he wasn't more upset with her. But he searched inside himself and found only...relief. Now, he knew what she'd been keeping from him. He understood the shadows in her eyes sometimes, the nagging sense that she'd been holding something back.

Hearing what that secret had been, that she'd second-guessed herself after being with him, was a weight off his shoulders. A worry off his mind. That, he could deal with. He could still see a way forward with her. And hell yes, he still wanted her.

"Are you…sure?" She placed a hand over his where he touched her cheek, holding his fingers captive while her eyes tracked his, searching for answers. "That is, yes, I would relive the memory with you. But it's still not fair to you since you don't remember us together."

Her "yes" rang through him, igniting a primal, chest-thumping roar inside. It felt like he'd been waiting for her forever. He'd hardly slept after the dinner at his house. After the meteor shower and the kiss under the stars. She'd invaded his every thought. Dominated his dreams.

"I've imagined it so many times, it's almost real." He tugged her hand to his lips and kissed the backs of her fingers. Lingered on the base of her thumb where he could feel her pulse race. "Besides, how many people get to have a 'first time' all over again?"

She tipped her head to one side, her hair falling away to reveal the vulnerable skin of her neck. More places he wanted to taste her.

"I'm not sure if we can top the *first* first time." Her fingers walked up his chest, slipping under the tuxedo jacket.

"I love a good challenge." His blood surged hot as he envisioned how things might have happened that night after he'd brought her home. "But tonight is going to have a whole different feel to it since we know each other better now. I've had a lot of time to think about us. To plot the best approach."

He brushed a kiss over the base of her throat and down to her shoulder, sweeping aside the strap of her silky gown for a better taste. She edged closer to him, her knee bumping his, her thigh pressing against him.

Heat seared him. He wrapped her in his arms, dragging her into his lap. She was so soft and fragrant, her hair and her dress tickling and teasing when he wanted to strip everything away and sink inside her.

Already, her fingers were at the fastenings on his shirt. He shrugged out of his jacket for her and realized they'd never pull this off here, on the couch. At least, not the way he wanted.

Lifting her in his arms, he carried her toward the only bedroom in the place. He knew the layout. But there was also something familiar about stepping into the darkened bedroom with her. Almost as if the memory wanted to surface.

For a moment, he chased it. But then, what did it matter compared to the here and now?

Gently, he set her on her feet. She'd kicked off her shoes at some point, her bare toes visible in the moonlight slanting through the blinds. He wanted to see her better, and he reached back to flick the wall switch that worked the fireplace here.

Another action that felt familiar.

"Brock?" Hannah's hand stilled on his chest; his shirt was already half off. "Are you okay?"

He fought off the déjà vu that wasn't real since he didn't remember that first night with her. Instead, he focused on her lips swollen from his kiss. Her dress already sliding off one shoulder where the strap had fallen, a hint of pink lace visible along with the curve of her breast.

Hannah waited, breathing in the scent of Brock's aftershave, a woodsy spice that she knew would make her knees weak for the rest of her days. He seemed on board with being together, but it worried her that his hand had gone to his temple. A pain? It hadn't been that long ago that he took a blow to the head.

"I'm better than okay," he assured her, lifting both her hands and twining his fingers through hers as he kissed his way down her neck. "I'm so damned good I might die from it."

His words vibrated along her neck, sending ribbons of pleasure down her back and making her skin tingle. Her breasts pebbled, the heat between her thighs impossible to ignore.

Just like the first time. Things were getting out of hand so fast she couldn't even keep track of all the ways he made her feel delicious. Feminine. Wanted.

Before she could ask for more, he was unfastening the other strap on her dress, lowering the bodice and feasting on one taut nipple right through the lace bra she wore. Sensation coiled tighter. Hotter. She gripped his shoulders, nails digging in lightly before she caught herself and eased up.

With a growl, he shrugged the rest of the way out of his shirt, his chest a pure pleasure to see and touch. Her hands roamed all over him, feeling every inch while he unzipped the rest of her dress. When the silk pooled at her feet, she tipped him back on the white duvet, falling on top of him and pinning him to the mattress.

For a moment, he watched her in the firelight, his blue gaze tracking her every move as she kissed her way down his chest to trace the muscles of his abs.

Hannah hadn't expected their new first time together to be even more intense. But it was. Mind-blowingly so. And she intended to savor every second of it.

She worked the clasp of his belt with anxious fingers while he unhooked her bra with a clever flick. She took all new pleasure from the feel of his hot skin against her bare breasts as she slid off his pants. His boxers.

But then, a new light flared in his eyes, his shoulders tensing as sweat rose along his back. He flipped her so that she was beneath him, pinning her there while he kissed her. And kissed her.

When both of their breathing had turned ragged,

he pulled himself away long enough to find a condom in a pocket of his jacket. She didn't wait for him to undress her. She eased the lace panties down with a swivel of her hips and a little help from one hand, savoring the way he watched.

Desperately hungry to have him.

He sheathed himself, and she was so incredibly ready. He kneed apart her thighs, positioning himself between them, driving himself...home.

The cry she made was a sound she didn't recognize, a throaty moan of completion when they were only just beginning. She wrapped her legs around him, losing herself in him. In this moment.

In a "first time" that, yes, was even better than the first time.

She stroked her fingers through his hair, whispering in his ear how much she liked every single thing he did to her, asking for more, giving him everything in return.

The sensations heightened even when she thought they couldn't possibly go higher. Her heels dug into his hips, her arms wrapping around him to hold him close. When he reached between them to stroke the juncture of her thighs, right where she needed him most, she went utterly still. A riot of sensation crashed through her, waves of pleasure coursing so hard she could only close her eyes and hold on.

Before she could even think how to give him that incredible sensual gift in return, he found his own peak. His thighs tensed, his shoulders and arms going rigid with the same bliss that had rolled over her.

She kissed his neck and chest, clinging to him. Lost with him.

She hadn't imagined he would possibly give her a second chance after the secret she'd kept from him, but the real possibility of more with him tantalized her now. Defenses nonexistent, she let herself feel all the delicious aftermath of being with him. The secret, joyful hope that this could be…everything.

When he rolled to her side, taking her with him to lie next to him, she tucked into his chest as if they'd been sleeping together for a lifetime. The rightness of the moment surrounding her, she savored the first sense of total well-being since the night her sister came home in tears.

The memory struck a painful note, but she pushed it to the side, promising herself she was going to find a way to avenge Hope. If anything, she felt stronger than ever in the shelter of Brock's arms.

Surely Hope would understand how much Brock meant to Hannah, and give her blessing to share the last of the secret Hannah had kept from him.

She was everything he ever wanted.

Even in his dreams, Brock relived the night with Hannah. The haze of slumber and sensation drew him deeper in, immersing him in her with an intensity that made him loath to wake up…

He lifted her in his arms, skimming off the scrap

*of blue lace around her hips before he pulled her
down to the white duvet with him.*

*She made soft, sexy sounds of approval in his ear
as she speared her fingers into his hair and drew
him down to kiss her. Shadows flickered across the
bed beside them in the firelight, the need for her—
for this—ratcheting higher.*

*He'd never bedded a woman so fast. Never imag-
ined a night like this where desire smoked away
reason and sensual hunger roared with predatory
demand. But Hannah was right there with him, her
hands shifting lower to smooth down his chest, back
up his arms. All the while she urged him faster, whispering soft commands to touch her. Taste her.*

He couldn't get enough of her...

Waking with a start, Brock glanced down to see
Hannah asleep by him, her blond hair covering her
shoulder like a blanket. He eased aside the strands to
stare down at her in sleep, the remnants of his dream
still clinging to the edges of his memory.

Their night together had been incredible. But as
his gaze snagged on her pink lace panties on the end
of the bed, he thought back to his dream. He'd been
so sure they were blue.

He could picture them perfectly. Bright, peacock
blue.

Even her bra had been blue.

Not pink.

Head aching, a rush of images assailed him. Of
a horseback ride with Hannah. She was wearing a

dark T-shirt, a black ball cap and a pair of leggings that helped him to feel every nuance of her curves when they'd been on the horse.

It wasn't a dream. It was reality. A memory.

He remembered.

The realization was so welcome, such a relief, he nearly woke her up to share the good news. Except that, with his memory came a sucker punch that landed squarely in his chest.

He'd gone to see her on set the morning after their first time, specifically to ask her about her guarded reaction to learning his name. He recalled vividly that Hannah had been upset to learn he was a McNeill. Why?

He'd asked her point-blank.

She hadn't been honest with him then. And she sure as hell hadn't told him the whole truth now. As much as he wanted it not to matter—it did.

Shifting away from her, he needed to get to the bottom of it. Before he could wake her, however, his cell phone vibrated on the nightstand. Lifting it, he saw a text from his oldest brother, Cody.

The words on the screen couldn't have shocked him more. The private investigator the family had hired wanted to talk to Hannah.

Twelve

"Hannah." Brock heard the ice in his voice but was powerless to fix it. Soften it. The realizations about Hannah were too damning. "We need to get dressed."

Already stepping out of bed, he had no choice but to slide on his tuxedo pants and shirt from the wedding.

"What's going on?" she asked sleepily, sitting up in bed, the sheet clutched to her.

"Two things." He buttoned the tuxedo shirt with impatient fingers, needing to get outside into the fresh air. Clear his head. "First, Cody asked us to come to the Black Creek Ranch main house. There have been some developments in the blackmail case, and apparently the private investigator has asked to speak to you."

He watched as she came fully awake, her face draining of color. "Me?"

"Yes." He grabbed his shoes and headed for the door. "And in other news, I've got my memory back."

He didn't wait to hear her reaction or her explanations. He couldn't process what was happening or why she was doing this to him, drawing him back into her life when she had purposely tried to distance herself from him after he'd gotten amnesia. Right now, all he could think about was getting to his brother's house fast and finally getting to the bottom of the scandal, the blackmail and—most painful of all to him personally—Hannah Ryder's deceit.

An hour later, the whole family had gathered in Cody's great room. It had cathedral ceilings and a stone fireplace that went up to the second floor, the room's tall windows letting the morning sun in on three sides.

Brock stood at the window while his brothers spoke in low voices with Dax, the private investigator who'd taken over the legwork on the blackmail investigation for the family. Hannah had attached herself to Emma and Jillian as soon as they'd arrived, which was just as well since Brock couldn't think of a single thing to say to her until he knew what was going on with the investigation.

She still hadn't been honest with him. Even after

the performance she'd given the night before—the insistence that she had come clean with him. Why had she even bothered when she was still withholding information?

She'd pulled on black leggings and a long gray T-shirt and tucked her hair in a ponytail before they'd left. She was sharing a cushioned ottoman with Emma near the fireplace. Madeline and Maisie put out some of the food they'd planned to serve at today's post-wedding breakfast for out-of-towners—pastries and sweet rolls—along with coffee and fruit. Not that Brock was hungry. But the scent of cinnamon and dark roast hung in the air from the kitchen island that lined one side of the great room. His father helped himself to a plate while they waited for Scarlett and Logan, the last to arrive. As the pair walked in the door, Dax—an Ironman competitor who used his digital forensics background in his work as an investigator—strode to the middle of the room.

"Thank you all for coming." The guy looked like he hadn't slept. There were shadows under his eyes, and his gray T-shirt and jeans were both wrinkled. "To bring you up to speed, the police arrested Emma's mother, Jane Layton, last night for trespassing on the Black Creek Ranch property."

Brock turned to look at Carson's girlfriend where the stuntwoman sat beside Hannah. Hannah squeezed Emma's hand while Carson stood behind her, his hands on her shoulders. Judging by her calm expression, Emma already knew about her mother's arrest. And now that Brock's memory had returned, he recalled meeting her, as well as her announcement that she feared her mother was the blackmailer. He had no idea why she believed that, however. He'd left his father's house early that night, unable to make sense of anything with his amnesia.

The investigator flipped pages in a notepad, his eyes scanning the small pages as he continued. "Jane is being held in custody as a person of interest in the blackmail case, and I'm close to having some additional evidence to share with police. But before I delve into that, Paige and Donovan have asked me to reveal a few things about Paige's past to help orient you."

Behind Dax, Cody was ushering his pregnant girlfriend into a chair at the kitchen counter and sliding a plate of fruit in front of her.

Seeing his brothers both so damned happy and in love only underscored the hole burning in Brock's chest this morning.

"Eden Harris voluntarily left home at age seventeen with the help of her stepmother, Stella Ventura." Dax nodded at Paige before turning back to the rest of the family. "Stella covered for her absence by assuring Eden's father, Emilio, that she'd left with her mother, Barbara. Stella also helped Eden disappear by putting her in touch with someone who gave her new identification papers and Social Security number so that she could become Paige Samara."

Brock was glad to learn of the logistics. He'd wondered how it was possible for a seventeen-year-old heiress to vanish, but clearly, his stepmother had help. His gaze drifted to Hannah, wondering if any of this was a surprise to her, or if she'd already known. Resentment simmered at the thought she may have used him to get close to his family.

Cody spoke up from his place near Jillian. "Paige has asked that we respect her privacy about why she left, and we're going to do that. Dad's lawyers are already working with a government agency to help her avoid any legal trouble since she used the false name and Social Security number under duress. But we thought it was important that we all understand who helped her to leave, and who was aware of her new identity, since that narrowed the field of possible blackmailers."

Close to where he stood, Brock noticed Scarlett's thinly veiled impatience. She shuffled from one foot to another and looked ready to speak until Logan King slid an arm around her waist. She seemed to settle down then, tucking close while the investigator took over the story.

Dax paced in front of the fireplace, his leather loafers creaking softly in the quiet as he tugged a pencil out from the wire ring of his notebook. "No one knew about Eden's new identity but Stella and, Stella realized afterward, her maid Jane Layton, who had overheard some of what transpired the day Eden left home."

Brock's focus shifted to Hannah in time to see

her bite her lip. Did she know something? But just then, Emma squared her shoulders and sat forward on the ottoman.

"My mother has battled bipolar disorder since I was very young," Emma explained. "I've always known she had an affair with Emilio Ventura, Paige's father, but I wasn't aware until recently that she tried to tell Mr. Ventura that I was his daughter. That's definitely not the case, by the way. I bear a strong resemblance to my father, who passed away a long time ago. But I think my mother might have tried to taunt Mrs. Ventura with the affair and with the idea that I could be Emilio's biological child."

Behind Emma, Carson shook his head. "None of that gives Jane a motive for blackmailing the McNeills, though." He cast a thoughtful glance over toward Paige. "Unless she thought Paige would pay to keep her secret quiet?"

Paige appeared unruffled. Relaxed even. Brock wondered if having her secret finally out had given her a new sense of peace. Certainly, she seemed happier than he could ever remember seeing her.

She finally weighed into the discussion. "Carson, I'll tell you what I already explained to Dax. I have no memory of Jane, either by sight or even by name. You have to remember, I was only a teen at the time, and I didn't grow up in my father's house. I simply stayed there for a few years when my mother was unwell."

"I met him, Mom," Scarlett blurted, straightening from her spot beside her actor boyfriend. "Your father, that is. And for what it's worth, I think he really misses you."

The two of them stared at one another, a silent conversation going on between them that Brock didn't begin to understand. Frustration built inside him; his shoulders pulled tight as he ground his teeth. He was tired of waiting for answers.

"So where does that leave us? Is Jane the blackmailer or not?" He was being abrupt, maybe, but his family had been dealing with too much these last weeks. Hell, *he'd* been dealing with too much trying to recover from amnesia while his family publicly fell apart at the seams. "And what does Hannah have to do with any of it?"

He heard her quick intake of breath, even from the other side of the room. No doubt he was still far too in tune with her, too aware of her every move. Breaking that bond was going to hurt, but it would be critical to moving forward.

Dax gave him a level look, a hint of displeasure on his face. Perhaps Brock had upset the guy's flow. Or maybe he'd wanted to speak to Hannah privately. But whatever it was, Dax recovered quickly enough.

"Much of what we have to tie Jane to the blackmail scheme is circumstantial, but it will be stronger once we eliminate any other possible connections between *Winning the West* and the Ventura family." Dax pointed to Scarlett's boyfriend with the chewed end of his yellow pencil. "Logan King has already spoken with me at length about his experiences with Antonio Ventura, and he has a firm alibi to clear him. The only other person with access to both the Venturas and the McNeills, as well as an interest in the movie, is Hannah Ryder."

All eyes turned toward her.

For a moment, Hannah wondered if the investigator would have tried questioning her in front of the whole group if Brock hadn't practically encouraged him to do just that. Not that it mattered. Helping her sister had somehow connected her to a blackmail investigation, and she couldn't impede a criminal case because of Hope's need for privacy.

She just wished she didn't have to speak about it in front of the whole family.

It hurt even more knowing that she was in this position because a man she'd trusted with her heart didn't trust her at all. But if she allowed herself to think about that now, she wouldn't be able to keep her composure through the questions. She was keeping herself together now by only sheer force of will.

"I can explain." Hannah stood, nervous energy making her want to pace. Or fidget. Her acting training wouldn't allow her to give in to that impulse. She understood the nuances of body language. "I was actively researching the Ventura family two months ago, and I briefly worked with a temp agency cleaning their home. I saw photos of Eden Harris and her mother in Emilio Ventura's study, and Jane Layton made an unusual remark about them that helped me link Eden with Mrs. McNeill."

"Why would you research the Ventura family?" Brock asked tightly. "You never mentioned that last night."

Hannah heard the disdain in his voice. Brock thought she was deceitful. A liar. And that hurt after what they'd shared.

Swallowing back the pain, she focused on the investigator instead. "I can explain why I did that, but since my story involves someone else, someone who wouldn't want her name mentioned, I would ask that you let me share the rest of it privately."

She waited for Dax's reply, prepared to answer his questions to the best of her ability. Maybe it would even be a relief to share with someone. The stress of what Hope had gone through had eaten away at both of them this year.

When the investigator nodded his approval, Brock crossed his arms over his chest.

"How convenient."

His cold words froze her feet to the hardwood floor, preventing her from following Dax into the dining area.

Mute with hurt and an anger of her own, she stared him down in front of his family. Willing her jaw to unclench, she said, "Excuse me?"

"You don't think I deserve to know what else you've been hiding from me?"

Before she could answer, Paige McNeill stood.

"Brock, please. Has it ever occurred to you she might need to protect someone?"

Gratitude filled Hannah's chest, a soothing balm, even if it would never fully ease the hurt of Brock's mistrust. Blinking away the sudden threat of tears, Hannah looked over at Paige. Really looked at her.

And something in the set of the older woman's chin, the tone of her voice, even the wringing of her hands, made Hannah think of her sister. It was a flash. An instinct. But in that moment, she knew without question why Eden Harris had run from the Ventura home. Why Eden had become Paige Samara McNeill and never looked back.

She'd been hurt once, too. By the same bastard who had hurt Hope.

"Thank you, Mrs. McNeill," Hannah murmured, hurrying past them to follow the PI into the dining room on the other side of the huge foyer. At the threshold, she paused, her heart thumping. She glanced back at the room full of Brock's family. And at Brock himself.

He stared out the front window, his expression inscrutable. He hadn't followed her, giving her the space that his stepmother had wanted him to. Hannah understood she'd hurt him. That in protecting her sister, she'd done deep damage to her fledgling relationship with someone she really cared for.

And maybe she'd done all she could to protect Hope now. She'd protected her sister's privacy as much as she could, even when it cost her a chance at something that could have been…so much more. Later, she would call Hope and ask for her forgiveness. Her understanding. But now, Hannah called back to the man she'd given her heart to, offering him the answers he craved. Already knowing it was too late for them.

"Brock?" She watched as his head came up. Their gazes locked, and his detached expression killed her a little inside. The hurt of what they'd lost left her breathless as she called back to him, "You're welcome to join us."

Maybe a better man would have simply trusted her, taking it on faith that her secrets were her own and didn't have any bearing on their relationship.

But Brock had been burned before. Not just by his ex-girlfriend, but by Hannah herself. Just yesterday she'd admitted she'd been lying to him. How was he supposed to take today's revelation that there were even more holes in her story? That she had some kind of connection to the Ventura family that she'd never mentioned.

So hell yes, Brock followed Hannah into the dining room, taking a seat near her as she began talking to the PI.

The story that came out made him half wish he'd never heard it. Not because the truth implicated Hannah. Far from it. His stepmother had understood the subtext of all that Hannah hadn't said, and as Hannah spelled out Antonio Ventura's crimes against her younger sister, the shattering facts made Brock fear what his stepmother had gone through living in the same household as Antonio.

It became all too clear that Antonio's sister—related only through adoption—had probably been his first sexual assault victim. And over twenty-five years later, the bastard was still getting away with taking advantage of young women who didn't have the resources or support system to take on a powerful man.

His first instinct, before Hannah had even finished giving her account, was to rally his brothers and inflict as much damage on Ventura as possible. But he knew that wasn't the way to stop a serial predator. Furthermore, he'd implied a level of discretion and respect for Hope Ryder's privacy by even setting foot in the room with Hannah as she spoke to the PI.

Now, like Hannah before him, he carried the weight of an ugly truth that wasn't his to share. But he would do everything in his power to leverage his resources and influence in a way that would help convince women to come forward. Perhaps even starting with his stepmother.

But first? He needed to find a way to talk to Hannah. To make some kind of amends for his lack of trust. Judging by the way she fled the dining room as soon as the private investigator assured her he had enough information, Brock didn't think she was going to give him that chance willingly.

Damn it.

He stood up fast, following her out into the living area. His father pointed wordlessly to the front door. And, out the huge windows, Brock could see her blond ponytail bouncing as she hurried away from the house with determined steps.

He needed to follow her. To apologize for not having faith in her. But first, he needed his whole family to understand one thing.

"Carson." Brock slid out of his dress loafers from the wedding, and grabbed a pair of boots by the door, not much caring who they belonged to. "I know you signed a contract with that movie production company. And it's fine if the movie films here, but not as long as Antonio Ventura is attached to the project. If he remains the director, we're going to shut the whole thing down, whatever the cost."

Donovan nodded tersely from his spot on the couch beside Paige, his arm tightening around his wife. "I will pay for the lawyers. Hell, I'll finance a whole army of them if that's what it takes."

Brock wondered how much his father knew about the director of *Winning the West*. He guessed Donovan didn't know the full story either, or Antonio would have met with a mysterious hunting accident a week ago.

"Thanks, Dad." He spared a quick glance at Paige, and a spear of guilt cleaved him in half for all the time she'd spent leading a quiet life, out of the spotlight, when she'd been an heiress in her own right.

She'd been in hiding from a monster for too long, and it was going to end now.

He stepped over to the couch long enough to lean down and press a kiss to his stepmother's cheek. "You were right about Hannah. I love you, Mom."

Then, turning on the heel of his borrowed boots, he headed out the door, determined to find Hannah—and find a way to make things right between them.

Thirteen

Hannah had ridden over to the Black Creek Ranch with Brock, so she had no choice but to walk back to her cabin.

Not that she minded. She welcomed the fresh air after the intense family meeting with the investigator and then, the more private discussion with Dax while Brock listened. Telling Hope's story had taken a lot out of her, but she was glad to have shared the truth. Now, she planned to pack her things and fly home as soon as possible.

Her sister didn't want her here anyhow, and she was worried about leaving Hope alone for much longer. If quitting the film ruined her career in acting, she truly didn't care. She would rather go broke fighting a legal battle to break her contract than spend another day taking orders from her sister's molester. Being in Wyoming this week had given her a taste for the life she'd rather be living anyhow. One that involved midnight stargazing and walks in the country. Horseback rides.

Her heart ached at the thought of that. She knew she'd never have a ride quite like the one she'd had with Brock.

"Hannah, wait."

The voice behind her was unexpected. And feminine.

Not that she planned to see Brock before she left, but she certainly hadn't cultivated personal ties with anyone else in his family.

Hannah shielded her eyes to see Brock's youngest sister, Scarlett, hurrying toward her. They had spoken briefly at the wedding the day before, just enough for Hannah to learn that Scarlett was excited about her move to Los Angeles and starting her own career in acting. Hannah had invited the younger woman to stay in touch after the filming ended in case she needed any advice. They'd do a lunch date.

And while the offer had been heartfelt, Hannah didn't think she could make small talk with her heart breaking. As Scarlett reached her side, Hannah turned to keep walking.

"I'm sorry, Scarlett, but I need to get back home." She stared down at the worn tire tracks she was following, grass encroaching on both sides. Cicadas made a high-pitched buzz while the sun beat down. "This morning has left me wrung out. Empty."

"My brother was out of line back there." Scarlett doubled her pace in order to keep time with Hannah's determined march.

"He's entitled to his opinion." She blinked at the burning in her eyes. Beneath her feet, the grass got blurry and she cursed herself for crying over something she couldn't change.

"Not when it's so wrongheaded." Scarlett took her hand and gripped it tight, forcing Hannah to stop unless she wanted to drag Brock's sister with her. "Men aren't always on our wavelength. At least, my brothers aren't. Brock can tell you the kind of mood a horse is in the moment he walks in the barn. But a woman? Not so much."

Hannah laughed. It was a watery yelp without much humor, but she appreciated Scarlett's attempt to defuse the tension. "He's great, actually. I screwed up by trying to hide things from him."

"I get it." Scarlett dug in her bag for a tissue and passed it to her. "And my mom obviously understood what was going on back there, too, which scares me."

"I think she ran away from home because of him."

"Antonio," Scarlett clarified. "His father even admitted to me that he's always worried his adopted son was a 'bully' and that's why Eden never returned home."

"I'd call him far worse than a bully, but I really can't share any more—" There was a vibration under her feet that surprised her. Then a horse and rider came into view from around a bend.

Brock sat tall in the saddle on Aurora's back, his tuxedo shirt open at the neck, the sleeves rolled up to his forearms, his black dress trousers tucked into dark leather boots. Her thoughts, and her gaze, stayed glued to him.

"Hannah." Scarlett squeezed her hand to get her attention. "I just wanted you to know that I'll talk to my mother. She's not a scared seventeen-year-old anymore. She's a woman of considerable power if she'll step up and own it. And I feel sure she will."

Hannah tore her eyes away from Brock. "What are you saying?"

Scarlett gave her a level look. She had a feminine flair in her dress, and an almost girlish beauty with her curls and wide blue eyes. But there was an absolute certainty about her, a grit and pride that only a fool would mistake.

"I'm saying Paige McNeill is an heiress two times over, and her word will carry weight in the court of public opinion. If we can get her to condemn Antonio, it's going to be vindication for whoever you're trying to protect."

Hannah thought about what she was saying. If Paige spoke out against Antonio, shared her own story, it could be career-ending for the director. Hope would see some justice served even if she never brought charges.

But maybe, if she saw others speak out against him, she would, too.

In her peripheral vision, Hannah saw Brock dismount the horse and begin walking their way.

"That would be…amazing," Hannah admitted, nerves jangling at the thought of talking to Brock. "Thank you."

It would make her trip to Cheyenne well worth it if she accomplished what she'd set out to—to let the world know that Antonio Ventura was a sorry excuse for a human being who did not deserve his vaunted place in the film industry.

Scarlett gave her an encouraging smile before backing up a step. "I'm going to start my campaign with Mom right now."

Brock's sister stalked off in the direction she'd come from, toward the ranch house that was now out of sight. That left Hannah very much alone with the man who'd condemned her in front of his whole family.

"I'm leaving," she told him, stuffing the tissue that Scarlett had given her into the pocket of the drapey, gray yoga shirt she'd thrown on this morning with her leggings. "I think that will be best for both of us."

She had fresh clothes on while Brock wore his recycled tuxedo shirt and pants, yet he still managed to look like a brooding lord out of a Jane Austen novel.

"That won't be good for me at all, Hannah, and I'm sorry that I've put you in a position where you feel like that would be best for you."

He sounded so sincere. And maybe he was. But it didn't change the things that had happened between them. It didn't mean he would ever trust her.

She dragged the toe of her running shoe through the grass, thinking she was going to miss the wide-open spaces here. The never-ending blue sky. She wished Hope could have seen it.

"In the end, we had different loyalties. My family had to come first for me. They—she—always will." She felt teary again and she needed to keep walking. Keep moving. "I'm in a hurry to get back now that I've made the decision. Do you mind if we continue walking?"

Brock whistled for the horse and the mare followed at an easy pace, nosing in the grass now and then.

"I know I overreacted today," he told her as they strode deeper into the wooded area along the creek. "Everything has been so intense this week. Ever since we met, I've had a scandal hanging over my head, and a blackmailer to catch. Then, the amnesia made it ten times harder to be any help to my family when they needed me most. So when my memory came back this morning and it still felt like you'd left things out, I didn't handle it well."

"You're protective of your family. I'm protective of mine. It put us at odds today." And that broke her heart as she thought of what could have been between them if things had been different.

"It wouldn't always." He snapped a dead branch

from a nearby tree and tossed it deeper into the woods, away from the trail. "That is, it doesn't have to."

She weighed the words as she allowed them to sink in, wondering if she was understanding him correctly, unable to squelch a flash of hope. Hope was scary, too, because she wanted to be a part of his life, to have more of those horseback rides and nights under the stars with him.

"I don't know what you mean." She picked up her speed, wishing she could outrun the hurt of losing him.

"I admire that you put your family first, even at the cost of you and me." He bent sideways to pick a tall Indian paintbrush, never slowing his step. "But how many times in a life does something like this come up? How often would family put us on opposite sides?"

Hannah shook her head. "Maybe never. But what does it matter when we've already broken this fragile thing we were building? When you've already shown me how quick you are to not believe me? You threw me under the bus back there, Brock."

"Like an idiot," he agreed, his boots following the worn path of one tire track while she remained on the other, a strip of high grass between them. "But just so you understand, I was thinking of my family, too. I assumed you were an enemy to the McNeills when the investigator wanted to ask you about the blackmail scheme. I didn't believe that for long. And if I'd had more time to think about it, I would have known you'd never hurt my family."

She thought about that, trying to see things from his perspective. Wondering where all of this was leading.

"So you want to call a truce? Shake hands before I leave and part on amiable terms?" She stopped walking, needing answers. "Please tell me what you hoped to accomplish by following me out here, Brock, because—in spite of what you think—I have no love for secrets. I'd prefer we speak plainly. Put our cards on the table."

Behind them, Aurora stopped to nuzzle through some grass. Hannah watched her because it was easier than looking at Brock, with his dark whiskers shadowing his jaw. She had too many memories of last night every time their eyes met.

"You want it plainly," he said. "Here it is."

She felt the soft brush of flower petals against her cheek as he encouraged her gaze. When she turned to see him, he tucked the stalk of Indian paintbrush in her pocket.

"I let one bad relationship color the way that I saw you, Hannah, and I'm sorry." He stepped closer as they faced off across the tall grass. "I pride myself on never making the same mistake twice, though, so if you could ever find it in your heart to forgive me and give me another chance, I promise I'd never hurt you that way again."

A bird chirped an optimistic song overhead, urging her to take a chance. To feel hope, and maybe even happiness.

The pull was so damn strong. Brock looked at her like she was the only woman in the world who mattered to him. The temptation to believe him, believe in the two of them together, was heady stuff.

"Let's suppose for a second that I did that. I said, okay, we'll try again." Her chest filled with too many feelings just saying the words aloud. Talking to him about this was like lifting the lid on Pandora's box and she was afraid she'd never be able to leave once the conversation started. She shook her head, willing her voice to stay strong. "What would that even look like? Hope lives in Los Angeles and she needs me there. You're a successful rancher with livestock and family who need you here. I just don't see a way to try."

And even as she said it, she found herself hoping he had the answer to make it all work. She couldn't deny that she wanted him in her life.

Brock lifted her hands, taking one in each of his. "Those are logistics. We can work around those. And if it came down to you and Hope wanting to be on the West Coast, I will gladly find a way to be there with you. The quarter horse program won't end if I leave the ranch."

"You would do that for me?" She thought about it for a moment, trying to picture that.

"Without a second thought."

"I never really thought about moving Hope here, though. She might actually be open to a fresh start."

The months of therapy hadn't helped. Maybe a move would give her sister a chance to heal.

"We don't need to decide today. I can fly back and forth until you're sure. But, Hannah, I promise, we could make it work." He squeezed her hands gently in his. "Maybe you could start by calling your sister. See if she wants to visit Cheyenne, just as soon as we get that bastard Ventura off McNeill lands forever."

"I'd like that. And I think Hope would, too." Hannah wanted to close her eyes and hold that vision tight. Hope here with her, finding peace in this beautiful land while she grew strong again. Except if Hannah closed her eyes, then she wouldn't be looking up into the eyes of the man she loved, and she wanted to keep that vision, too.

"Like I said, those are things we can figure out as we go. What matters is if we want to—that is, if *you* want to—try. I already know how badly I want to." He kissed the back of one hand. Then the other. "I'm in love with you, Hannah."

His words shot through her confusion with the precision of Cupid's arrow. The intensity in his blue eyes made her breathless.

"I'm in love with you, too," she admitted, shaking her head, the worries sliding away in light of that one simple fact. "That's why this all was hurting so much."

Relinquishing her hands, Brock wrapped his arms

around her and pulled her against him. The tightness in her chest eased, giving away to the warmth of a happiness so full and sweet she thought she might overflow with it.

"I don't want to ever hurt you again," he promised, kissing her hair, her forehead and then, tilting her chin up, her lips. "I'll do whatever it takes to make you happy, and to help keep your sister safe."

She smiled against him, her teeth nudging his as a happy laugh bubbled up. "I trust you to keep that promise."

She wound her arms around his neck, pressing herself fully to him, giving herself over to the kiss.

They lost themselves in it, mouths moving together, until they were both breathless, the promise of a future together stoking passion higher inside her. She gripped his shirt, certain of what she wanted.

A forever with Brock McNeill.

He eased away slowly, tipping his forehead to hers.

"So we are in agreement." He stroked her shoulders, warming her all over with one simple touch.

"Perfectly. I'm going to call Hope just as soon as we get home." She wanted to phone Scarlett, too. She had the feeling Brock's sister was going to be an amazing champion for Hope's cause. "Maybe we can go on horseback?"

Her gaze slid to Aurora, remembering that first night with Brock.

His wicked chuckle told her that he remembered every delicious detail, too.

Epilogue

Nine months later

Hannah's bags were packed. She finished zipping one of the designer suitcases that Brock had given her for Christmas, her brain full of lists and preparations for her first week away from Hope since her sister had moved to Cheyenne with her last fall.

"Are you sure you have everything?" Hope asked from her seat at Hannah's dressing table, where she'd plopped herself with her tablet to oversee the packing. Hope had been working on a screenplay for the past two months, her thirst for writing returning in what her therapist called a good sign of her emotional recovery. "That doesn't look like enough luggage for a Hollywood movie premiere and a vacation in wine country. You're living the McNeill lifestyle now, Hannah. You deserve some extra luxuries," she teased.

Hannah looked into her sister's eyes, grateful every day she saw the spark of happiness flaming brighter and brighter there. Of course, Hannah had a lot to be grateful for lately. Antonio Ventura was facing prison on harassment and molestation charges. To date, over fifty women—including Hannah's friend Callie—had come forward to add their voices to the case after Brock's stepmother had shared her story with the police.

Hope hadn't wanted to share hers publicly yet, and the therapist said they needed to respect her journey. Hope told Hannah she felt vindicated enough that he was behind bars, and she seemed to be thriving in Cheyenne, taking a part-time job exercising horses at the Creek Spill while she completed college classes online. She'd talked about returning to campus next fall, but for now, she had her own suite in Brock and Hannah's home.

"I just don't have the diva instinct, I guess." Hannah had found a joy in the simpler rhythm of the days on the ranch, developing a special affinity for the cowboy boots that had been Brock's "housewarming" present for her when she agreed to move in.

Like Hope, she found plenty to keep her busy helping out with Brock's quarter horses, especially keeping the website updated with photos of the animals in training, and tracking each animal's progress for interested buyers. Brock had said those stories had led to more and better sales for the ranch, so she was contributing. But like her sister, she was contemplating a second act. For Hannah, it might be in producing. She had a strong interest in bringing female-driven stories to the big screen, and it was a job that would give her flexibility, too. Something she'd need for the family she and Brock had talked about.

Hope shut off the screen on her tablet and set it on the dressing table, folding one foot underneath her. "It's funny that you—a former Hollywood actress—moved to Cheyenne and forgot how to be a diva. While Scarlett—a rancher's daughter—moved to Hollywood and has made a name for herself as the Diva Cowgirl."

Hope was referencing Scarlett's popular social media account that had attracted followers around the globe. Scarlett and Logan King were still a hot item, and Scarlett's date nights always made great photo ops. If Brock wanted to know what his youngest sister was up to, he asked Hope, who could show him up-to-the-minute photos from Scarlett's account.

But there was far more to the Diva Cowgirl than great clothes and glitter makeup. Scarlett had been instrumental in Antonio Ventura's downfall, leading the charge against him in the media. Hannah loved her dearly.

"Diva or not, you'll notice she still comes home most weekends," Hannah reminded her, wanting to plant it in Hope's head that she could return to Cheyenne as often as she liked if she decided to move back to Los Angeles.

"That's mostly because of Charlotte," Hope added, sniffing one of Hannah's perfume bottles. "She's gaga over Cody and Jillian's new baby girl."

Their child was a double blessing since Jillian was a breast cancer survivor who had thought she'd never have children. Mother and baby were both thriving, and shortly after Charlotte had been born, Emma and Carson announced they were expecting, too. Emma had been glowing with happiness when they'd revealed the news over a Sunday dinner with most of the Cheyenne branch of the McNeill family.

Sadly, Emma's mother had turned out to be Paige's blackmailer, but Jane Layton had been found unfit to stand trial and, according to Emma, seemed more at peace now that she was receiving additional care for previously undiagnosed mental health issues.

"Of course she's thrilled. We're all excited for the baby," Hannah agreed just as Brock stepped into her bedroom.

"Who's having a baby?" Brock asked, dressed in a blue suit and white shirt with no tie, more handsome than any Hollywood leading actor, in her opinion.

But then, this was the man who made her heart beat faster with just a look. Like the one he was giving her now. The one that said they shared a secret. Hannah felt warm all over and was grateful when Hope answered for her.

"We're talking about your brother's new baby. Charlotte is too adorable for words, and I think I'll go visit her if you two can ever get out the door to catch your flight." Hope hopped to her feet, heading for Hannah's luggage. "Want me to carry a bag down?"

Laughing, Brock strode past her, gently taking the bag from her hands. "Not a chance. One of the stable workers is going to load the car for me and drive us to the airfield."

"Really?" Hope looked interested and headed for the door. "I hope it's Chad. He's the cutest." She was already hurrying down the hall to look out the front window.

"Are you ready, Hannah, my love?" Brock asked, taking both her hands in his and helping her to her feet. "Are you prepared to go see the premiere of *Winning the West*?"

The production company had done extensive re-shooting of the film after Antonio was fired as the director. Hannah had to admire that they hadn't wanted their name—or the film—tainted by association, so she'd stuck it out and reshot her scenes with the new director.

"Now that I'm officially proud to have my name attached to it, yes." She stood in front of him, letting her body graze his, tempting them both with what they would share tonight. "Mostly, I'm looking forward to having you all to myself for a few days."

"How am I going to keep my hands off you in the car ride to the airstrip?" he whispered in her ear, releasing her hand so he could splay one of his along her back.

"Not to mention on the plane." She eased back a step, her arms looped around his neck. "Maybe I'd better behave."

"The plane won't be a problem," Brock assured her. "Didn't I mention we're taking my grandfather's private jet?"

The McNeill patriarch continued to be generous to his Wyoming relatives, flying them all to his spring wedding to Rose Hanson. Hannah had never attended a more romantic ceremony than the union of the dapper octogenarian to the feisty former Harlem torch singer. They were a perfect match.

Hannah smiled, toying with the hair at the nape of his neck. "You didn't say one word about a private jet, Brock McNeill, or I would have remembered."

"It's the first of many surprises I've got planned for you this week," he assured her, his gaze dropping to her lips before he slanted his mouth over hers and kissed her with slow, heart-melting thoroughness.

She would have forgotten about the trip if he had kept going. He still did that to her.

"Do you want to see another one of the surprises?" he asked.

Intrigued, she angled away from him to see his expression. His blue eyes were full of warmth. Love.

He'd kept his promise to make her happy, that's for sure.

"Okay," she said. "Yes."

He reached into his jacket pocket and withdrew a small, velvet box.

Her heart did a backflip. Her gaze was glued to this unexpected gift.

"I think we've really covered the logistics of being together," he told her, his voice serious. Sincere.

"Me, too." Breathless, she remembered that conversation with him nine months ago when she'd first trusted him with her heart.

"These months with you have been the happiest of my life, Hannah. I can't imagine spending another minute without you, knowing how much I want to be with you forever. How much I want to have a family with you." He dropped to one knee in front of her and opened the box as he took her left hand. "Will you make me the happiest man ever and marry me?"

She wasn't sure if the tears in her eyes were making the round diamond look like a huge, glowing crystal ball, or if it was simply that magnificent. But it seemed to emit a light all its own, sparkling with promise in a simple platinum band.

There wasn't a single doubt in her mind.

"Brock, you've made my dreams come true." She wrapped her arms around him again, dragging him to his feet so they could hold each other. She laughed and cried and kissed him all at the same time. "Yes, I can't wait to marry you."

She felt the sigh of relief rocking through him as he hauled her to his chest. His heart beat fast, too, letting her know just how important this was to him.

Their love was a deep, incredible gift. They held each other close for a long moment.

From outside the bedroom, Hannah heard a car horn and her sister shout that their ride was here. Hannah didn't move, though. Not yet. She kissed Brock again with all the love in her heart, knowing their story together was only beginning.

* * * * *

*When tech billionaire Benjamin Bennett returns home
for his cousin's wedding, a passionate weekend with his
former crush—his elder sister's best friend
Sloane Sutton—results in two surprises. But can he get
past Sloane's reasons for refusing to marry him
for the twins' sakes?*

Read on for a sneak peek of
The Billionaire's Legacy *by Reese Ryan,
part of the* Billionaires and Babies *series!*

Benjamin Bennett was a catch by anyone's standards—
even before you factored in his healthy bank account.
But he was her best friend's little brother. And though he
was all grown-up now, he was just a kid compared to her.

Flirting with Benji would start tongues wagging all
over Magnolia Lake. Not that she cared what they thought
of her. But if the whole town started talking, it would
make things uncomfortable for the people she loved.

"Thanks for the dance."

Benji lowered their joined hands but didn't let go.
Instead, he leaned down, his lips brushing her ear and his
well-trimmed beard gently scraping her neck. "Let's get
out of here."

It was a bad idea. A really bad idea.

Her cheeks burned. "But it's your cousin's wedding."

He nodded toward Blake, who was dancing with his

bride, Savannah, as their infant son slept on his shoulder. The man was in complete bliss.

"I doubt he'll notice I'm gone. Besides, you'd be rescuing me. If Jeb Dawson tells me one more time about his latest invention—"

"Okay, okay." Sloane held back a giggle as she glanced around the room. "You need to escape as badly as I do. But there's no way we're leaving here together. It'd be on the front page of the newspaper by morning."

"Valid point." Benji chuckled. "So meet me at the cabin."

"The cabin on the lake?" She had so many great memories of weekends spent there.

It would just be two old friends catching up on each other's lives. Nothing wrong with that.

She repeated it three times in her head. But there was nothing friendly about the sensations that danced along her spine when he'd held her in his arms and pinned her with that piercing gaze.

"Okay. Maybe we can catch up over a cup of coffee or something."

"Or something." The corner of his sensuous mouth curved in a smirk.

A shiver ran through her as she wondered, for the briefest moment, how his lips would taste.

"What's the worst that could happen?" Wyatt asked.

I could get hurt.

Except Lindy didn't need anything from Wyatt. Nothing but his body, anyway. If, in theory, she were to give in to their attraction. He couldn't take anything from her. Not her house, not her land. And if she didn't love him, he couldn't take her self-respect, he couldn't take her heart, and he couldn't give her any pain.

Really, what was the point of going through the trauma of ending a ten-year marriage if you didn't learn something from it? If she knew this was only going to be physical, only temporary…

What was the worst that could happen?

"I…"

He leaned in, his face a whisper from hers. And oh… The way he smelled. Like sunshine and hay. Hard work and something that was just him. Only him.

She wondered if he would taste just the same.

She was about to find out, she knew. He was leaning in, so close now.

She wanted… She wanted to kiss him.

She wanted to kiss another man, finally. To take that step to move on. But more than that, she wanted to kiss Wyatt Dodge more than she wanted to breathe.

And bless him for taking the control. Something she never thought she would think, ever. But he was going to take the decision away from her, and she wasn't going to have to answer his questions, wasn't going to have to do a single thing other than stand there and be kissed.

She was ready.

He squeezed her chin gently, pressing his thumb down on her lower lip, and then he released his hold on her, taking a step back. "Think on it," he said.

"I… *What?*"

But he was already moving away from her. "Think on it, Lindy," he said, turning around and strolling away from her.

She looked around, incredulous. But the street was empty, and there was no one to shout her outrage to.

And damn that man, she still wanted him to kiss her.

***

Good Time Cowboy
by New York Times *bestselling author Maisey Yates,*
available September 2018 wherever
HQN Books and ebooks are sold.

www.HQNBooks.com